THE WIZARD OF WAR SMOKE

Marshal Matt Fallen and his deputy Elmer Hook have never seen War Smoke so busy. People are gathering for the opening night of the Tivoli theatre, and top of the bill is the famed Mezmo, an illusionist who can reputedly mesmerize anyone into doing his bidding. When a series of murders occurs before the show begins, Fallen is convinced that Mezmo is to blame. But as more men fall victim to the mysterious assassin, can Marshal Fallen outwit the Wizard of War Smoke and discover the truth behind the slayings?

MICHAEL D. GEORGE

---◆---

THE WIZARD
OF
WAR SMOKE

Complete and Unabridged

LINFORD
Leicester

First published in Great Britain in 2016 by
Robert Hale
an imprint of The Crowood Press
Wiltshire

First Linford Edition
published 2020
by arrangement with
The Crowood Press
Wiltshire

A catalogue record for this book is available
from the British Library.

ISBN 978–1–4448–4441–2

Published by
Ulverscroft Limited
Anstey, Leicestershire

Set by Words & Graphics Ltd.
Anstey, Leicestershire
Printed and bound in Great Britain by
T. J. International Ltd., Padstow, Cornwall

This book is printed on acid-free paper

Dedicated to my friend Clint Walker and his lovely wife Susan.

Prologue

The Diamond Pin hotel towered over most of the other buildings along Front Street. It boasted eighteen rooms of various sizes but only three that faced the wide thoroughfare and the multitude of people which traversed its length. One of those rooms was occupied by notably the best poker player in the sprawling settlement.

Holt Berkley, professional gambler, had owned the hotel for the eighteen months since he had successfully drawn to an inside straight. That solitary hand of stud poker had made Berkley one of the richest men in War Smoke.

Yet, as with all professional card players, he had never been able to stop risking every cent he possessed by submitting to his addiction.

As the sky grew ever darker and the street lanterns were lit along Front

Street, casting their amber illumination across its churned-up sand, Berkley struck a match and ignited the gas lamp in his private room. He adjusted the flame to fill the room with light before blowing the match out and dropping its blackened length into an ashtray.

The gambler parted the lace drapes and looked down at the street. So many differing souls moved in all directions below his first-floor vantage point. So many suckers, he thought. All of them had their weaknesses and he had made his living for nearly ten years by exploiting them.

Berkley had been wealthy before he had obtained the Diamond Pin. When War Smoke was no more than a tented city he had arrived, just ahead of the barber and slightly after the wagon of whores.

He had erected a canvas tent and began selling over-priced whiskey and playing poker. Within six months he had made enough money from his patrons to build a wooden structure to replace his original tent. Now, from his hotel window, he could see the Red Dog gambling hall standing proudly halfway along Front Street. The gaming house had never shown a loss in all the years he had owned it.

Yet with all his wealth, Berkley still had a craving to play poker, even though he had more money than he could spend in a dozen lifetimes.

Tonight he had prepared the hotel room for a private game of stud poker. He had invited three of the town's most powerful people to join him and was expecting them to arrive at any moment.

A knock sounded on the door behind him. Berkley walked around the card table and gripped the brass doorknob. He turned it and pulled the door towards him.

The hallway was shrouded in darkness. The famed card player was puzzled. He stepped out and looked up and down the corridor in search of his guests.

He pulled a box of matches from his colourful vest pocket, withdrew one of the long sticks and moved towards a gas-fitting on the wall.

'I could have sworn someone knocked my door,' Berkley muttered. He struck the matchstick along the side of the box and raised it to the gas jet. He returned the matchbox to his pocket, turned the gas on and allowed the flame to ignite the pungent gas. As he blew the match out he touched the small glass globe to adjust the light.

To his surprise the globe was hot.

'That's mighty odd,' he muttered. He turned round and looked in both directions along the hallway. All of the other wall lights were off. 'The lamp must have bin on just like they're all meant to be. Somebody has turned off all the lights. Why?'

It was a question to which he would never learn the answer, for as he was about to enter his room again he caught sight of a shadowy figure at the end of the hall.

Berkley's hand reached for his .45. He squinted at the shadow. He could make out a figure moving towards him slowly like a phantom. His finger curled

4

around the weapon's trigger and he gritted his teeth anxiously.

'Who is that?' he called out. 'Show yourself.'

The shadow moved towards the light until it became corporeal to his straining eyes. A smile stretched across Berkley's face as an unwarranted sense of relief filled his soul.

He removed his hand from the six-shooter and ran his fingers through his slicked-down hair.

'You scared me there for a moment,' he said as the figure edged out from the darkness and then stopped barely three feet from his side. Slowly, as the flickering gaslight danced across the features of both men, Berkley realized that something was wrong.

The gaslight danced on the barrel of a small gun in an outstretched hand. The gun was aimed straight at the gambler.

Berkley's expression altered to one of panic as he focused on the small-calibre gun. He was about to speak again when suddenly the sound of the weapon discharging reverberated along the corridor.

The card player felt the impact of the bullet as it cut through his vest and continued until it found his heart. He rocked on his highly polished shoes, then he folded. His knees hit the boards and he wavered there for a few seconds. Droplets of blood dripped from the neat wound and splashed on to the floor.

The gambler had lost his fair share of many poker games in his time but none of those defeats had been like this. This time he knew that he had lost his very life.

He watched his executioner depart along the corridor and vanish into the depths of the hotel's shadows. With blood pouring from the hole in his chest made by the perfectly aimed bullet Holt Berkley fell forward on to his face, his fingers clawing at the boards.

Finally only involuntary twitching came from the poker player as the last dregs of life evaporated from his outstretched form.

His convulsing body gave out a sickening rattle as blood flowed from his mouth.

A couple of hundred yards along Front Street the sound of the single shot caught the attention of the two lawmen inside the marshal's office.

'What in tarnation was that, Marshal Fallen?' Elmer Hook asked the tall lawman as the sound of the shot echoed around the office like a lost thunderclap.

Matt Fallen rose from his chair and strode towards the open door where his deputy was standing and scratching his head. He looked in both directions, then reached back and snatched his Stetson off the hat stand.

The marshal stepped out on to the boardwalk and frowned as he vainly looked around the lantern-lit street. He pulled his hat over his head of dark hair.

'That was a shot, Elmer,' he said. His large hand rubbed his neck in frustration. 'But where the hell did it come from?'

Elmer walked to his boss's side and gazed up at the sky. 'Reckon you're right, Marshal. It sure don't look like there's a storm brewing anywhere close to War Smoke.'

Fallen glanced at his deputy. 'It seemed to me as though it came from inside one of the buildings along Front Street, Elmer. A shot out in the street would have sounded crisper and louder by my reckoning.'

The deputy looked confused.

'Maybe it weren't a shot,' he suggested. 'Usually a gun being fired draws more shots after it. That was a darn lonesome noise.'

The tall marshal stepped to the edge of the boardwalk. His eyes searched for answers. He was beginning to doubt his seasoned instincts. He rested a hand on the porch upright and sighed.

'You're right, Elmer,' he agreed. 'Maybe my nerves are a bit on edge.'

'Why don't you catch forty winks in one of the jail cells, Marshal Fallen?' Elmer gestured at the marshal's office.

'You ain't slept in two days. You're plumb tuckered out.'

Fallen nodded and turned. 'Well, I was kinda busy guarding that gold shipment before we saw it off on the train this morning.'

Elmer reached up, placed a hand on the lawman's shoulder and patted it.

'Go and get some shuteye,' he advised. 'I'll wake you up when it's time for us to do the rounds.'

The deputy's offer was too tempting to resist. The marshal was about to walk back towards the open office door when the familiar voice of Doc Weaver caught his attention. He stopped and looked down the lantern-lit street at the face of his oldest friend as the medical man hurried breathlessly towards them, clutching his medical bag in his ancient hands.

'Matt,' Doc repeated over and over again until he reached both the watching lawmen.

Fallen and Elmer waited as the elderly man with the small black bag in his grip caught his breath and eventually straightened up.

'What's eating you, Doc?' Elmer asked.

Marshal Fallen steadied Weaver. 'You do look fired up, Doc. How come?'

'Somebody's bin shot, Matt,' Doc gasped, panting like a hound dog. He squinted up at both lawmen. 'Didn't you hear the damn shot?'

Fallen nodded and turned a raised eyebrow in his deputy's direction. 'We heard something, Doc. I figured it was a shot but we couldn't work out where it came from.'

Doc looked at the marshal. 'It came from the Diamond Pin, Matt. Bobby the bell-boy come running to tell me that some pitiful critter is lying in a pool of his own blood.'

Fallen gritted his teeth and frowned.

'Then what are we waiting for?' he said.

The three men ran down the long wide street towards the Diamond Pin. They hurried through its large doors and crossed the lobby to where a pale-faced clerk stood shaking behind his desk.

Fallen rested his hands on his gunbelt and leaned over the desk. His eyes narrowed.

'Just give us a clue where we might find the varmint with the bullet hole in him, will you?' he growled.

'Up the s-stairs towards the f-front, Marshal,' the clerk stammered, his left hand pointing the way. 'I've never seen so much blood.'

'You'll see a whole lot more if you hang around this town, sonny,' Doc told him grimly and trailed Fallen and Elmer up the stairs to the landing.

Fallen moved his muscular frame around the landing until he noticed one of its corridors was unusually dark. He moved to the corner and looked to where only one gas lamp was lit, halfway along its length. The lifeless body of Holt Berkley lay in a crumpled heap, bathed in flickering gaslight.

The marshal glanced at Doc.

'I found the body, Doc,' he drawled. 'C'mon.'

Doc and Elmer followed the marshal through the dim illumination to where Berkley's body lay beneath the wall light. While Doc and Elmer both knelt beside the motionless body Fallen walked into the hotel room and stared at the green-baized table set in the centre of the room surrounded by four hardback chairs. He moved towards it and noted the poker chips and several decks of cards neatly stacked around the circumference of the table. A plentiful supply of whiskey bottles rested on a desk near the window.

'It looks like someone was going to have themselves a few hands of poker,' Marshal Fallen said. He turned to look back at his companions. 'Have you any idea who that dead varmint is, Doc?'

Doc looked up at his tall friend. 'I sure do. This is Holt Berkley, Matt.'

'Glory be, Marshal Fallen,' Elmer gasped. 'It sure is Holt Berkley. Somebody's up and killed him.'

12

'Berkley?' The lawman walked back to where his friends were kneeling and stared down at the body cradled in Doc's arms. 'Hell. That *is* Holt Berkley.'

'Was,' Doc corrected.

Elmer stood and looked at the curious expression on the marshal's face. 'What you thinking about, Marshal?'

'I'm trying to work out who would kill Holt Berkley, Elmer,' the marshal replied. 'And why?'

'That surely is a real puzzlement.' Elmer shrugged as he looked nervously to both ends of the dark corridor. 'I sure hope that gun-toting critter is long gone. I don't cotton to go joining Mr Berkley at the pearly gates.'

'Don't go fretting, Elmer,' Doc said with a sigh. 'I reckon the odds of you getting to the pearly gates are mighty slim.'

The deputy looked even more confused. 'Is Doc joshing with me, Marshal Fallen?'

The marshal shook his head. 'I don't reckon so, Elmer. I don't think you've got any chance at getting to the pearly gates either.'

Doc stood up and wiped the blood off his hands on the sides of his old jacket.

'There ain't nothing I can do here.' He sighed again. 'You'd best call for the undertaker, Matt.'

The marshal nodded in agreement, then rubbed his neck with the palm of his left hand as his mind raced. Something just did not add up in Fallen's mind. He knew that gamblers always made a lot of enemies but most of them would settle their grievances before they left the card table. He had never heard of any losing card player killing like this before.

It did not make any sense. Fallen turned on his boot heel and looked at the card table once again.

'That card table is set up for four players. Berkley was expecting three guests by my calculations.'

'Holt must have bin intending playing for big stakes to have himself a private game,' Doc reasoned. 'That means his three guests are well-heeled.'

'You're right, Doc.' Fallen nodded.

'Do you figure that one of them killed him?' Doc asked, closing his black bag. 'Mind you, it looks as if none of them has arrived yet.'

'Could have bin a robbery, I guess,' Fallen said. 'If you're gonna rob someone, Holt Berkley would be my first choice.'

Something protruding from the back pocket of Berkley's pants caught Elmer's eye. The deputy reached down and pulled a swollen wallet from the trousers. He straightened up and opened the large billfold.

'This weren't no robbery, Marshal Fallen,' he suggested as he showed the thousands of dollar bills in the leather wallet to his friends. 'Berkley had himself a small fortune on him and it's still here.'

'Why would his killer not take the wallet?' Doc said. 'That's mighty strange.'

'That's damn strange, Doc,' Fallen

agreed. 'It means it's fairly certain the killer came here with only one intention and that was to execute Holt. He had no intention of robbing him at all.'

'Well, g-glory be,' Elmer stammered. 'Mr Berkley was murdered pure and simple. Some varmint intended killing him and done it.'

Fallen rested his knuckles on his hips. 'But why didn't he take the wallet? Even the highest-paid gunman would have taken his wallet to add to his fee.'

The deputy's eyes widened as he shuffled closer to the two older men.

'What if it was a ghost, Marshal Fallen?' Elmer suggested innocently. 'They don't need money like living folks.'

Doc lowered his head and shook it. 'Give me strength. How many ghosts you ever heard of haunting folks with a six-shooter, Elmer?'

Fallen took the wallet from the deputy and slid it into the inside pocket of his vest.

'I'll put this in the office safe until we figure out what to do with it,' he said.

'Have you got any notion as to what this is all about, Matt?' Doc wondered as he shuffled towards the window of the room.

Fallen shook his head. 'Nope, not yet.'

Elmer looked up and down the dark corridor. 'Do you figure some *hombre* turned off the rest of these gaslights, Marshal Fallen?'

'Yep, I sure do. Now you can light them again, Elmer,' he instructed the deputy. 'I want this hall lit up like high noon. There might be something along here that we ain't found yet. A clue that might give us an idea who killed Berkley.'

Doc edged closer to the marshal. His wrinkled eyes looked up at the towering lawman's face.

'What's going on here, Matt?' he wondered.

'Damned if I know, Doc,' Fallen drawled and patted his old friend on the shoulder. 'But I intend finding out. This killer ain't gonna get away with cold-blooded murder in my town.'

17

Doc looked out of the window at Front Street and War Smoke's latest attraction. The Tivoli saloon had been closed for months while a small fortune had been spent upon it to turn it into a theatre. Two torches blazed on either side of the entrance.

'The Tivoli is opening up again tonight, Matt,' Doc noted. His hands patted his pockets until they came across his pipe.

'I know.' Matt Fallen nodded. 'Me and Elmer got us two free tickets to attend.'

The medical man pushed the stem of his pipe into the corner of his mouth and struck a match above its well-filled bowl.

'Are you going?' he asked.

Fallen shrugged. 'Depends on how busy I am.'

'I ain't.' Doc gripped the stem of his pipe between his store-bought teeth. 'The last thing I need is so-called entertainment. A few glasses of rye down at the Longhorn will be enough excitement for me tonight.'

With every gaslight illuminating the hotel corridor Elmer strode towards his two friends with a large grin on his face.

'You oughta go, Doc. I hear tell they got dancing gals and sword-swallowers and even knife-throwers. I'm plumb excited.'

Doc shook his head.

'Sounds a little too cultured for me, Elmer,' he wheezed.

Noticing that the pipe had stopped billowing out clouds of smoke from its corncob bowl, Matt Fallen scratched a match with his thumbnail and offered it to the old medical man. As Doc rekindled his tobacco the marshal continued to stare across the street at the Tivoli.

'I wonder if any of those performers know anything about this killing, Doc?' he pondered.

Doc eyed Fallen as he puffed on his pipe. 'I was wondering about that myself.'

The broad-shouldered marshal looked at his deputy.

'Go and get Sam the undertaker,

Elmer,' he said. 'Tell him we got a new customer for him.'

The deputy did exactly as he was ordered. The sound of his boots echoed through the hotel corridors.

'The town owes me two dollars for this, Matt,' Doc said, raising his bushy eyebrows.

'What for exactly?' the marshal enquired wryly.

'For pronouncing Holt Berkley dead.' Doc tapped his pipe stem on his teeth.

'I'll take it out of petty cash, Doc.' Fallen nodded. He continued to look across the wide street at the Tivoli, which was lit up like the Fourth of July.

'What you thinking about, Matt?' Doc asked.

'I'm thinking about paying the Tivoli a visit, Doc,' Fallen drawled. 'I've a notion I'll find the answers I'm looking for over there.'

1

Ten yards of seasoned lumber had been added to the rear of the Tivoli to provide the warren of dressing-rooms and props all decent theatres required to satisfy the performers they were luring from the eastern seaboard. The result was a shadowy labyrinth. People could move about behind the newly constructed stage without being noticed. They could also enter and leave the building by doors set on either side of the construction.

Although the marshal did not realize it yet, his gut feeling was closer to the truth than even he could ever have imagined. Stagehands mingled with the variety of performers as they all prepared for the grand reopening of the Tivoli. As with all such activities, organized chaos ruled. Raised voices held the hint of panic in their tones as the clock slowly ticked down to when the luxurious drapes must part and the show get started.

If, as Matt Fallen suspected, the deadly assassin was one of the newly arrived performers in War Smoke, he knew that he had his work cut out for him to prove it.

Undeterred, Fallen strode from the Diamond Pin towards the Tivoli with his pipe-puffing friend at his side just as the undertaker arrived at the hotel.

'You think that Elmer is gonna be OK back there, Matt?'

'Even Elmer can't hurt a dead man, Doc,' Fallen replied. He stepped up on to the boardwalk outside the lavishly decorated saloon and stopped to survey the building more closely. He was studying the billboard of performers as the elderly medical man caught up with him. Doc glanced at the saloon and shook his head.

'Beats me why they wanted to change this place, Matt,' he grumbled. 'Don't make no sense. If'n they wanted to spend money they should have built a clinic in case we get another outbreak of fever.'

'There ain't no profit in building a clinic, Doc,' Fallen answered wryly. 'This is progress.'

Doc spat at the sand. 'That's what I think of progress.'

Fallen looked at a billboard more closely and studied the acts it proclaimed. His eyes narrowed as they focused on the name at the top of the bill.

'Mezmo the Great,' he read aloud, scratching his neck whiskers. He glanced at his shorter companion. 'It seems to me that I've heard about him, Doc.'

Doc adjusted his small spectacles, looked at the name, then read the line below it.

''The greatest mesmerist in the world.'' Doc raised his bushy eyebrows and gave a chuckle. 'The critter ain't burdened with bashfulness, is he?'

Fallen noticed that the front doors were locked. 'We'll go around back and find another way in. I want to have a talk with some of these theatrical folks.'

The lawman and his elderly companion walked beyond the flaming torches to the corner of the Tivoli and made their way down an alley at the side of the building. The dimly lit alley led them to a side door. A solitary lantern above the door cast its amber light down upon the two men.

Doc looked at the extension. 'This is new, Matt.'

'Yep.' Fallen removed his Stetson and moped his brow with his sleeve. He then returned his hat to his head and pulled the door open.

'What do you figure it is?' Doc asked.

'This must be where they keep all them 'artistes' corralled, Doc,' Fallen guessed. He sighed as he wondered if he would ever get the scent of the murderer in his nostrils.

'Do you think we're allowed in there?'

'I'm going in anyways. C'mon, Doc.' The tall marshal pulled the door further towards the tin star on his vest. He led the old-timer from one kind of starlight to another.

The smell of greasepaint greeted them. Both men stood for a moment amid the dressing-rooms as their eyes adjusted to the strange illumination. The lamplight was dim but well positioned. The door of each of the dozen small rooms had its own oil lamp attached at one side.

The marshal and doctor listened as countless voices washed over them from the dressing-rooms and the backstage area. A volatile mixture of laughter, anger and panic came from every angle as the confused pair looked at each other.

'What kinda place is this, Matt?' Doc wondered as they both caught fleeting glimpses of dancing girls in various states of undress. Only the shadows provided them with a fig-leaf of modesty as they scurried between the dressing-rooms. Matt Fallen smiled as his eyes feasted on some of the shapely females.

'Whatever it is I'm sure glad we didn't bring young Elmer with us, Doc.'

Doc chuckled. 'Might have stunted his growth.' He nodded.

'I often wondered what happened to make you so short, Doc.' Fallen smiled as he led his flustered friend past the various dressing-rooms. 'Now I know.'

Doc trailed the lawman as Fallen read the notes which were pinned to the wooden doors.

'Are you looking for anything in particular, Matt?' he asked.

'I'm trying to find Mezmo, Doc,' Fallen answered his puzzled companion. 'Don't you remember? That *hombre* interests me.'

As Doc passed the open dressing-room doors and his watery eyes accidently feasted on the scantily clad females he lifted his hat and repeated:

'Howdy, ma'am. I'm a doctor.'

At the very end of the line of dressing-rooms, Marshal Fallen stopped abruptly. The little Doc bumped into him and looked apologetic. The lawman glanced down at his blushing friend.

'Are you OK, Doc?' he asked. 'You're mighty red.'

'Why'd you stop for?' Doc asked.

The tall lawman pointed at the note pinned to the only closed door in the line of dressing-rooms.

'This is Mezmo the Great's dressing-room.'

Doc looked at the room. A large paper star had one word scrawled upon it. Mezmo.

'How come it's the only one with the door shut, Matt?'

Fallen gripped its handle. 'This door is bolted. I also wonder why his door is the only one that ain't open?'

'What you so all fired up about him for, Matt?' Doc asked as the marshal raised his hand to knock.

Fallen paused and glanced down at his friend.

'I'm not sure, but I'm curious about mesmerism,' he answered. 'I've heard that some folks can actually use mesmerism to put people into a trance and make them do their bidding. Others reckon it's all just a trick to fool the audience.'

Doc stroked his wrinkled face with

27

his fingers. 'I'm one of them doubters, Matt. It seems to me that it ain't possible to take control of another critter's mind.'

Matt Fallen looked into his older pal's eyes.

'Would you let someone try to mesmerize you, Doc?' he asked.

'I sure wouldn't,' Doc answered sharply. 'I might be wrong. I'd hate to find myself in an embarrassing situation.'

'I figured as much.' The lawman clenched his fist and was about to rap his knuckles across the door when the unmistakable sound of a gunshot resonated throughout the Tivoli. Fallen stopped and swung on his heel. 'Did you hear that?'

'That was a shot, Matt,' Doc replied.

Matt Fallen's gaze darted around the shadows. 'Where'd you figure it came from, Doc?'

Before the medical man could answer the door to the alley swung wide open and the gangly figure of Elmer stood there, squinting in search of his superior.

'Marshal Fallen?' he called out. 'You

in here, Marshal Fallen?'

With Doc on his heels, Fallen strode through the the half-light and the bustling show people towards his deputy. He stopped beside the youngster and pushed the brim of his hat off his brow.

'What, Elmer?' he growled.

Elmer pointed over his shoulder frantically. 'Something awful has happened, Marshal. Lou Franklin has bin shot. Shot dead as best as I can figure.'

'Lou Franklin the banker?' Doc gasped.

'The very same, Doc.' Elmer nodded as his attention was drawn to several of the showgirls.

Fallen rubbed his upper lip as his mind once again raced at the news of another death in War Smoke.

'Are you sure about this, Elmer?' the lawman asked the deputy. 'Are you certain it was Lou Franklin?'

'It was him OK.' Elmer nodded. 'I nearly tripped over his dang body outside the Diamond Pin, Marshal.'

'Damn it all!' Fallen looked down at Doc. 'Two of the richest men in the territory get themselves killed within an hour. I've got me a feeling that Franklin was one of the men Berkley was expecting to play poker with, Doc.'

'You might be right, Matt,' Doc agreed.

Suddenly a sense of urgency came over the marshal. 'We'd best find out who the other two are and warn them before the murderer strikes again.'

Elmer was buffeted as both Fallen and Doc pushed past him and rushed out into the night air. The deputy had a pained expression on his face as he scratched his head and tried to keep up with events.

He turned to follow the marshal and Doc Weaver when a sharp voice with an unfamiliar accent stopped his progress. The piercing Bronx accent cut through the shadows and startled the deputy.

'Will you and your pals stop opening that damned door?' the female screeched as the young lawman glanced over his bony shoulder. 'There's a hell of a draught in here. Us dancers ain't got very big costumes, you know.'

A handful of performers had gathered in front of the dressing-rooms when the sound of the gunshot had shaken the wooden walls of the Tivoli. Most were females in various stages of undress. One of them pushed through the throng and pointed at Elmer.

'Do you hear me?' she continued. The lamplight was illuminating her shapely form.

'Golly gee!' Elmer gasped.

'What you smiling at?' the uninhibited female asked the astonished deputy. 'Ain't you ever seen a woman before?'

'I never seen as much woman before.' Elmer blinked hard as his eyes focused on the noisy dancer. His innocent grin filled his face as he staggered out into the alleyway and resumed his pursuit of his companions.

The deputy had nearly reached the front of the Tivoli when he stopped and looked back as he suddenly realized what his eyes had just witnessed.

'Holy smoke! That gal was buck

naked!' Elmer exclaimed excitedly. 'I'm definitely going to that show tonight. Not even that loco killer is gonna stop me.'

2

The lantern light from the hardware store window spilled over the dead body stretched out on his back across the boardwalk. Once again a single bullet had ended a life with devilish accuracy. Lou Franklin had been a man in his early sixties with more money than he knew what to do with. Like so many other men in his privileged position, the banker had sought ways to enliven his otherwise boring existence. For Franklin the solution had been playing poker with the town's elite for high stakes.

Losing at cards was almost a relief to the banker, and if he won the occasional hand it simply justified his love of the game. Yet now all Lou Franklin could do was stare up at the countless stars in the night sky with glazed, lifeless eyes.

This was a scene brutally replicated from their worst nightmares. Another dead body in the sprawling town of War Smoke was drawing curious onlookers like an outhouse attracts flies. The tall marshal waved them away with a stern look and an unspoken threat of them spending the night in one of his jail cells.

'Get going, folks,' Fallen drawled as Elmer crossed the wide street and headed towards him. 'There ain't nothing to see here.'

'You heard Marshal Fallen,' Elmer repeated, ushering the townsfolk away from the motionless body. 'Git going.'

As the crowd dispersed, Matt Fallen rested a hand on a porch upright and looked down upon the body whilst Doc checked over the corpse. The older man glanced up at the marshal's troubled face and shook his head.

'Poor old Lou must have bin dead before he hit the ground, Matt,' he stated. He closed his medical bag and stood back up. 'He was shot just like Holt.

Small-calibre bullet straight through the heart.'

'Damn it all!' Fallen cursed. 'What's going on here?'

Doc shook his head. 'Like it or not, Matt, we've got a killer in town and I've a feeling that he ain't through yet. How you gonna stop it?'

The lawman remained silent as Elmer walked up beside him. 'I cleared the crowd off, Marshal Fallen,' the deputy told his boss.

Fallen tilted his head. 'Did you happen to see who shot old Franklin, Elmer?' he asked.

The skinny deputy shook his head and placed a foot on the boardwalk. He looked sadly upon the banker stretched out in the amber light.

'No I didn't, Marshal,' Elmer replied. 'I'd just seen the undertaker's hearse off from the hotel and walked to the office to rustle up some coffee. Then I heard the shot and come running.'

'You didn't see anyone?' Doc queried.

The deputy shook his head. 'Who-ever shot Mr Franklin must have bin a phantom or something. The street was no busier than it is right now, Doctor. Whoever done this just melted into the shadows somehow.'

Doc checked his pocket watch. 'By my reckoning we've had two killings in less than thirty minutes, Matt.'

'It's only bin dark an hour,' Elmer said glumly.

Fallen clenched his fist and pounded the wooden upright angrily. The lawman wanted answers but no matter how hard he tried he could not find anything that seemed to make sense to his tired mind. He was more used to men blasting their six-shooters at one another or at him in plain sight.

Both Berkley and Franklin had been executed in cold blood with lethal accuracy. Whoever was unleashing their lead was doing so in a way Fallen had never encountered before.

It troubled the tall lawman.

'I can't figure this, boys,' he muttered

through gritted teeth. 'It just don't add up in my head. I've never known anyone kill like this.'

'You're dog tired, Matt,' Doc said, shuffling away from the body. 'Get some shuteye. Once you've rested up you'll be better fixed to figure this out.'

The lawman raised an eyebrow and shrugged.

'I can't do that, Doc,' Fallen admitted. 'The bodies are stacking up too fast.'

'At this rate we'll be up to our chins in dead 'uns before sunup.' Elmer looked along the wide street.

Fallen glanced at Elmer.

'Go and tell Sam we got another customer for his funeral parlour,' he ordered his underling.

As the deputy raced off down the street, Doc moved closer to the broad-shouldered lawman. He tilted his head back so that he could look up at Fallen's face.

'You got any objections to buying me a few drinks, Matt?' he asked. 'You look like you could use a few stiff ones yourself.'

Fallen nodded and turned to the doc. 'The town owes you another two bucks by my reckoning, Doc.'

'You ain't paid me the first two bucks yet, Matt,' Doc said and guided the marshal towards the Red Dog saloon.

'I ain't had time yet, Doc,' Fallen replied. 'Besides, the way things are going you're gonna make a fortune before I can stop this killer.'

The two men stopped to watch as the undertaker steered his hearse into Front Street and headed towards them. Fallen stepped down on to the sand and pointed at the body. Sam Jacobs drew rein and stopped his matched pair of chestnut geldings beside the remains of Lou Franklin.

'C'mon, Doc,' Fallen said as he placed a hand on the ancient shoulder of his friend. 'I'm buying us both a few drinks.'

The Red Dog gambling hall had ten card tables spread out from the bar counter, but only two of them were occupied as men played poker. Fallen led Doc to the bar and placed his boot on the brass rail as the medical man ordered the drinks.

The bartender placed two glasses of whiskey in front of them as Fallen tossed a silver dollar across the well-polished counter.

The two men had only just raised the whiskey to their lips when Elmer entered the Red Dog and walked up to where Matt Fallen and Doc were propped. He rested his hands on the damp counter and looked at his troubled boss.

'A beer for Elmer,' Fallen told the bartender.

'Sam's gonna take care of Mr Franklin, Marshal,' the deputy said. 'He said thanks for all the business.'

Fallen looked at his underling. 'I hope you told Sam that I ain't the one shooting folks, Elmer.'

Elmer pouted. 'I'm sure Sam knows that, Marshal Fallen. The bullet holes would be a whole lot bigger if you was doing the killing.'

Fallen rolled his eyes and downed his drink. He snapped his fingers for a refill as the bartender placed a beer glass with amber suds in front of the deputy. Elmer took a sip of the beer, then cast his attention around the saloon's interior.

'Ain't very busy in here, is it?' he observed.

Doc raised his eyebrows. 'I reckon most of War Smoke are putting on their Sunday best to go to the Tivoli later, Elmer.'

Fallen stared at his empty whiskey glass and pushed it forward. The bartender refilled the glass.

'And one for Doc,' Fallen said.

'Mighty generous of you, Matthew,' Doc acknowledged.

Fallen toyed with the small glass. 'I wish I could figure these killings out, Doc. I've tried to work out what's going on but I keep coming up empty. Who in tarnation is killing and why?'

'Marshal Fallen?' Elmer piped up.

'What, Elmer?' Fallen sighed and

turned his head.

'Can you tell me what a Mezmo is?' the deputy asked. 'I ain't never heard of a word like it. He must be real good to be the top of the bill though.'

Doc eased himself towards the deputy. 'You asking what a mesmerist is, Elmer?'

Elmer nodded. 'I sure am. Whatever he is, the poster says he's great. But great at what exactly? I ain't never heard them words before. What's this *hombre* do?'

'I hear tell that he puts folks in a trance, Elmer,' Doc said. 'Mesmerists tend to make folks do things they would never do unless mesmerized.'

The deputy looked even more confused.

'Well, thank you kindly. That's as clear as mud, Doc. At least they got dancing gals in the show. I seen me one and she was buck naked.'

Doc chuckled as Fallen downed his drink.

'I wonder who else Holt Berkley was waiting for?' the lawman said thoughtfully. He placed the glass down on the

41

bar counter. 'I'm heading back to the Diamond Pin to ask that jittery desk clerk a few questions.'

'That's a real good notion, Marshal,' Elmer agreed. 'I think I'll come with you.'

Fallen looked at Doc. 'Some men my age got themselves hound dogs but I'm saddled with Elmer.'

'I'd prefer a hound dog, Matt,' Doc grinned. 'They don't eat as much as him.'

The deputy looked offended. His brow furrowed as his gaze darted between the chuckling medical man and the broad-shouldered man with the tin star pinned to his vest.

'It ain't right for you to josh with me,' Elmer snorted. He finished his beer and wiped his mouth on his sleeve.

'Hush up, Elmer.' Doc laughed as he watched the lawmen head for the swing doors. 'I'll tell your ma about you seeing that buck-naked gal otherwise.'

Front Street was glowing in amber light but the brightest illumination was coming from the Tivoli saloon. It was a beacon that would entice even the most conservative of folks to enter it. The marshal glanced down the street to where the church stood in the reflected light of so many far smaller buildings. The clock on its tower could be seen from practically anywhere in War Smoke. Matt Fallen led Elmer across the wide street towards the hotel at a pace that defied his weariness.

'We've still got an hour before the show starts at the Tivoli, Elmer,' the marshal drawled. 'I've got me a gut feeling that when it kicks off all hell is gonna break loose.'

Elmer looked frightened.

'You do?' he stammered.

'One way or another I reckon that show has something to do with these killings, boy.' The marshal stepped up on to the boardwalk and walked straight through the open double doors into the bright hotel lobby as his deputy shuffled behind him trying to keep pace. Fallen did not slow his pace until he reached the desk and impatiently started to slap its counter with the palm of his left hand.

His pounding resonated around the lobby of the Diamond Pin as Fallen's eyes searched for the young desk clerk.

'Where the hell are you, boy?' Fallen shouted loudly. The young hotel clerk suddenly appeared on the landing and ran down the stairs to the desk. 'Where you bin, son?'

The clerk looked even paler than when Fallen had seen him earlier. It was obvious that he had been sick and he looked as though he was ready to throw up again.

'I've bin upstairs cleaning up all that blood, Marshal,' the queasy young man answered meekly. 'I figured that Mr Berkley would want the corridor clean.'

The marshal rested a hand on the desk and lowered his voice. 'Do you happen to know who your boss was expecting tonight?'

'I do.' The clerk looked nervous. 'What do you wanna know for, Marshal?'

Elmer stepped forward and pointed a finger at the clerk.

'Marshal Fallen wants to know because your boss and one of his buddies has bin shot dead,' Elmer said bluntly. 'Unless you want the other two critters' deaths on your conscience, you'd best tell him their names. Savvy?'

The young clerk looked up at the towering marshal and nodded meekly. He swallowed hard and edged closer to the desk. He leaned over the register.

'If you don't kick him I will, Marshal Fallen,' Elmer snorted. 'Tell the marshal, you young locobean.'

'Mr B-Berkley said it was a s-secret, M-Marshal,' the clerk stammered nervously. 'But I reckon it's OK telling you now. Him being dead, I mean.'

Fallen sighed impatiently.

'I'm waiting, son,' he said.

'Mr Berkley always played poker with the same three gentlemen every week,' the clerk informed the lawmen. 'Lou Franklin, Jed Silver and Seth Gordon. They were the only men rich enough in

War Smoke that could match him dollar for dollar, Marshal.'

Fallen turned to Elmer. 'The banker, the judge and the lawyer,' he said.

The deputy looked troubled. 'They're three of the richest folks in War Smoke, by golly,' Elmer added.

'They were,' Fallen differed. 'You forget that one of those three is dead, Elmer.'

Elmer nodded and ran his fingers through his greasy hair.

'We gotta find the judge and that lawyer and warn them, Marshal Fallen,' he urged his superior. 'We gotta find them fast before they end up in old Sam's funeral parlour with their buddies.'

The tall lawman rubbed his chin.

'You're right. They'll be the richest dead folks in War Smoke unless we can warn them, Elmer. C'mon.' Fallen spun on his heel and charged back out into the lantern-lit street with his deputy hot in pursuit.

'Where in tarnation are we gonna start looking, Marshal?' Elmer asked, desperately trying to keep up with the towering lawman. 'They could be anywhere in town.'

Fallen paused and looked down at his deputy.

'I reckon that the judge should be home by now, Elmer,' he said. 'Maybe we oughta start there.'

The deputy frowned. 'But Judge Silver lives on the far side of town in one of them big fancy houses. That's one hell of a walk and no mistake, Marshal Fallen.'

'Then let's get over to the livery and hire us some real fast horses.' Fallen patted the deputy on the shoulder and started to run through the amber lantern light. 'C'mon, Elmer.'

3

Attorney Seth Gordon had made his fortune as one of the best lawyers in the territory. It was said that it did not matter how many men you killed as long as you had enough money to hire Gordon to defend you in court. If the lawyer had ever lost a case, nobody could remember it. Rumour had it that Gordon used every underhand trick in the book to win his cases and his sheer audacity had made him far wealthier than anyone in his profession ought to have been.

Renowned for his oratory, the lawyer could literally talk the birds out of the trees. Some of the most hardened outlaws in the territory had willingly lavished their fortunes on the legal eagle just to ensure he would defend them in court.

But, like other men with more money

than they could ever live long enough to spend, Seth Gordon had found an addiction that he could afford.

Poker was his chosen poison.

Gordon had honed his natural skill as a card player while he was still a young man and learning his trade as a lawyer. He had spent three summers travelling up and down the Mississippi on the riverboats. By the time he had earned his shingle he was already a wealthy man.

Gordon was a modest drinker and required something to help him relax after defending his dubious clients. Poker was the only thing that he delighted in and his weekly tournaments with his fellow addicts had become the only thing that he looked forward to.

The lawyer adjusted the gold pin in his cravat and adjusted his jacket sleeves so that his matching gold cufflinks were visible. He placed his silken top hat on his head, then plucked his gunbelt from a coat stand and wrapped it around his waist. He secured the buckle and checked the Colt .45 in its holster.

Now he was ready to make the long walk from his office to Front Street and the awaiting Diamond Pin hotel. A wry smile wreathed his mature features as he locked his office door behind him and headed for the front door to the street.

The lawyer was still in the best of health and it showed. He descended the steps to the boardwalk with his ebony cane tucked under his left arm.

Gordon inhaled the crisp night air and started the familiar journey just as he had done hundreds of times previously.

The lights at the heart of the large town drew many creatures when darkness blanketed the settlement, but few were quite as wealthy as Gordon. He had heard the distinct sound of the two separate gunshots earlier but, like so many others, had ignored them.

The sound of occasional gunfire in War Smoke did not alarm the well-dressed lawyer. He was used to it. Every night shots were fired up into the heavens by various drunken cowpokes as they vainly attempted to extinguish the moon or shoot bats out of the air.

Seldom did the noise of gunplay mean anything more serious than liquored-up folks letting off steam. The lawyer continued on towards the profusion of street lights at his usual pace.

Although Gordon had heard the two solitary shots they did not linger in his mind. He had far more exciting things to consider. Would he be the one who finished the night with all of the coloured chips? he wondered. Gordon was not the best poker player in town but he had managed to extract several thousands of dollars from his fellow players the previous week and was eager to do so again.

The closer he got to the heart of the settlement the busier it got. Yet unlike on most nights when he made this journey it was not riders on horses he noticed but men and females on horse-drawn vehicles.

Gordon wondered what was going on

in War Smoke. He adjusted his hat and watched couples dressed as handsomely as himself begin to appear from their homes and make their way into the centre of town. Most were on foot but a number were readying their buggies.

The lawyer turned the corner from Baker Street and continued down towards Front Street. He instinctively patted his billfold in the inside pocket of his frock-coat and checked the holstered six-shooter on his hip.

Both wallet and .45 were loaded and ready for action.

Gordon strode purposefully on to where the street-lights glowed at their brightest. The private poker game at the Diamond Pin hotel was the highlight of his week and the only occasion on which he could relax.

As he continued on towards the hotel, he noticed that even more buggies were being readied. Again the keen mind of the lawyer was confused at the sight of so many elegant vehicles being prepared during the hours of darkness.

Then he recalled being told about the grand reopening of the Tivoli. Gordon realized that the refurbished saloon was opening its doors tonight.

He crossed the wide expanse of sand and turned the corner into Front Street. His narrowed eyes squinted through the amber light down at the very end of the long thoroughfare. He could see the alluring lanterns hanging from the Diamond Pin's porch overhang and smiled in anticipation. Then Gordon noticed the pair of blazing torches opposite the hotel. The sheer brilliance flooded across the distance between the two buildings, illuminating everything between them.

Front Street was getting busier by the second with every passing heartbeat. The slick lawyer smiled to himself as he noticed the crowd gathering in front of the Tivoli.

'That place is going to make a fortune,' he said. He paused and pulled a long thin cigar from his breast pocket and placed it between his lips. 'Shame I didn't buy shares in the place when I had the chance.'

Gordon scratched a match down a porch upright and cupped it at the end of the cigar. He drew smoke into his lungs and studied the impressive array of illumination. Had this not been his poker night he might have been tempted to find out what the fuss was all about.

He shook the match and tossed it at the sand.

'Reckon I'll buy a ticket for tomorrow night's show, but tonight I've got a date with my friends,' he whispered and exhaled a line of smoke into the air.

Gordon was about to start walking again when movement in the shadows in an alley that ran between two stores caught his attention. The lawyer's hand moved swiftly to the grip of his holstered Colt. He drew the weapon and cocked its hammer. His eyes searched the shadowy depths of the narrow alley. A few large boxes dotted along the six-foot-wide alley masked his view.

The lawyer took a few steps into the alley.

Unlike most men of his profession Gordon was a skilled marksman; he did not fear anyone. He moved further into the dimly lit alley and searched the area with narrowed eyes. Like so many other dark places in War Smoke the alley had the scent of a place where men emptied their bladders.

Again he caught sight of a shadowy figure. Gordon held the six-shooter at hip level and aimed it straight at the perplexing sight.

'You'd best show yourself,' he said powerfully, taking another step forward and vainly searching for the substance behind the elusive shadow. 'I get a tad nervous in dark places. Show yourself or I might start shooting.'

There came a slight noise directly ahead. The lawyer raised the .45 swiftly until he was able to look along the length of his outstretched arm through his gun sights.

'Don't even think about trying to best me, fella,' Gordon warned through gritted teeth. 'I'll blow your head clean off your shoulders if you do.'

Suddenly another aroma filled his nostrils. It was the scent of rosewater. The attorney felt a bead of sweat trickle down his temple from his hatband. Gordon raised an eyebrow and saw the figure moving towards him through the shadows.

He tried to work out whether it was a man or a woman, but it was impossible to tell. The figure seemed to be draped in black. Gordon swallowed hard and his heart pounded inside his chest.

'You're damn close to meeting your Maker,' the lawyer warned. His index finger stroked the trigger of his cocked Colt. 'One false move and I'll kill you. Do you savvy me? Do you?'

There was no answer.

The strange silent figure continued to glide towards Gordon as though it were a marionette controlled by some unseen puppet master.

'Why don't you say something?' Gordon snapped.

Once more his demands were greeted by silence.

Gordon continued to watch the eerie figure move closer and closer towards him. It was barely visible as it silently advanced from the depths of the blackness. Even as wisps of reflected lantern-light danced off the walls the lawyer still could not determine who he was aiming his .45 at.

It was only when the figure in black got within ten feet of Gordon that it become obvious what it was that the lawyer was actually looking at.

A sense of relief washed over the attorney. He sighed and lowered his six-shooter. A smile lit up his handsome features. He no longer felt threatened.

'I could have killed you,' he said. 'You had me mighty troubled there for a moment.'

The figure in black stood directly before Gordon. The scent of rosewater now filled the lawyer's nostrils as he held his Colt at his side. He released its hammer gently and holstered the deadly weapon.

Gordon tipped his hat.

'My apologies,' he said as his eyes vainly

attempted to focus in the half-light. 'When I heard the noise I naturally got spooked.'

There was still no reply.

'You don't say much, do you?' The lawyer took another step as his eyes finally focused on the stranger. 'My name's Seth Gordon. I was just on my way to play poker with a few of my oldest friends in the Diamond Pin. Reckon I'd best be on my way.'

The lawyer was about to turn when he heard something. He turned back to face the silent stranger. His brow furrowed and again his eyes narrowed.

'What was that noise?' he asked.

There was no answer.

Gordon caught sight of a small handgun as its nickel-plated barrel caught the lantern-light. Surprised, Gordon tilted his head and opened his mouth to speak.

But not one solitary word left his lips.

The sudden appearance of the small pocket gun as it rose up, its barrel aimed at the unsuspecting attorney, was too fast. Gordon was only six feet away from the six-shooter when his narrowed eyes spotted the .45's glinting barrel.

His eyes widened. Gordon went to draw his own weapon again. It was too late. He had barely grasped its ivory grip when a short sharp blast erupted from the small-calibre weapon like a miniature lightning bolt.

Gordon hardly felt a thing at first. He watched the shadowy figure turn and move silently back along the alleyway away from him. Within seconds the figure was gone.

Seth Gordon glanced down at his chest to where a neat bullet hole in his expensive shirt began to leak blood.

Only then did he realize that he had been fatally wounded.

Gordon tried to shout but all that left his mouth was gore. It poured like a scarlet river down his face. He coughed and clutched at his chest.

Blood spread through his fingers.

Gordon's watery eyes vainly searched for his assassin as he felt his life ebbing as the torrent of crimson gore continued to flow.

The lawyer gasped and staggered backwards.

His highly polished shoe heels caught the edge of the wooden boardwalk. Gordon toppled like a tree.

The lawyer crashed across the wooden walkway at the feet of passing townsfolk. With the light of countless street lanterns dancing upon his lifeless body, startled females began to scream at the sight of the dead attorney.

Within seconds the entire street resounded to the noise of their hysterical shrieking. Men rushed in response to the terrified cries to where Gordon lay in a pool of his own gore.

'It's Gordon the lawyer,' someone shouted in horror. 'He's bin shot.'

'He's dead!' another exclaimed.

The elegant attorney did not hear the words. He would never hear anything again, apart from the gentle strumming of harp strings.

4

The lawmen furiously lashed the rumps of their mounts and thundered from the heart of War Smoke along the leafy trail to where they knew the most affluent of the settlement's citizens resided. Neither the marshal nor his deputy had any idea what was happening in their town, but they realized that unless they stopped the killing soon more bodies would be added to the tally.

Darkness had brought death with it. For some reason they had yet to figure out an unknown assassin was hard at work dishing out his own brand of justice.

To the marshal it seemed obvious that the arrival of so many strangers in War Smoke was no coincidence. He was also convinced that every one of the four poker players were doomed unless he could find and stop the killer quickly.

The two saddle horses obeyed their riders and rode swiftly along the dark, unlit road to the outskirts of town. For more than twenty minutes the animals kept pounding along the dusty trail as they covered the distance between the heart of War Smoke and the lavish residences.

As the horses continued to gallop towards their goal, Fallen began to wonder if somehow the mysterious killer might have reached Judge Silver before them.

A cold shiver traced along his spine. He knew that the odds of finding the judge alive were getting slimmer with every beat of his pounding heart.

Finally his narrowed eyes spotted the array of house lights ahead of them. Fallen pointed a finger.

'There it is,' he shouted above the sound of their horses' hoofs.

The deputy nodded and leaned back against his saddle cantle. His bony wrists strained as he slowed his horse down. Then Elmer shouted out the very thing the marshal had been thinking only moments before.

'Do you reckon we're in time, Marshal?'

The senior lawman did not reply as he wrestled with his long leathers and pulled them up towards his chest.

Matt Fallen and Elmer pulled up their horses as they reached the most exclusive quarter of the sprawling town. The marshal dismounted and stared around the area as his deputy dropped from his saddle to stand beside him.

There were only a half-dozen houses in this area, far from the heart of War Smoke. Each of them looked far too splendid for honest folks to own.

Fallen looked troubled. 'All we gotta figure is which is the judge's house, Elmer.'

Elmer shook his head. 'That'll take hours, Marshal. That's time we ain't got.'

'I know,' Fallen agreed.

The deputy scratched his head. 'Where do we start, Marshal Fallen? Each of them houses is bigger than the livery stable.'

The marshal led his horse across the dusty road to where a few trees fringed the trail. He waited for his deputy to catch up with him before speaking again.

'We'd best start then,' he muttered.

'But which one of these castles do you reckon belongs to Judge Silver, Marshal Fallen?' Elmer asked, running his fingers through his hair while he studied the brightly illuminated mansions.

Fallen held the reins of his mount and sighed as he too tried to work out which of the properties looked grand enough for a judge to reside in. He tilted his head and looked at his deputy as the younger man tied his reins to a branch.

'We ought to get closer, Elmer,' Fallen said. He secured his own horse's leathers and cast his eyes along the line of grand dwellings. 'I reckon Jed Silver will have himself a mighty fine brass shingle on his gate.'

Elmer edged closer. 'You reckon, Marshal?'

Fallen exhaled.

'I sure do, Elmer. All the folks that figure they're better than the rest of us have shingles with their names on them, don't they?'

'Like the one outside Doc's?' Elmer grinned.

'Exactly.' The marshal walked across the dusty ground towards the first house. Sure enough there was a shingle on its wooden fence. Fallen struck a match and held it close to the fancy plaque. 'Told you so.'

'Well, if that don't beat all,' Elmer gushed. 'You done found the judge first time, Marshal.'

Fallen blew the flame out, tossed the spent match over his shoulder and started to approach the house. Lamplight spilled from its many windows, augmenting the amber light of the glowing lantern hung above the huge door.

'Correction, Elmer,' Fallen drawled as they neared the door. 'I found his shingle. We ain't located the judge yet.'

Elmer placed a hand on the marshal's shoulder. 'We will. I got faith in you, Marshal Fallen.'

'Well thank you, Elmer,' the marshal said and sighed.

The door was larger than any the pair of lawmen had ever encountered before. Yet its proportions matched those of the mansion perfectly.

'Well, if that don't beat all,' Elmer gushed again. 'You could drive a stage-coach through this door if'n it was open. Why'd you reckon he needs a door this large for?'

'Saves him money if he happens to put on weight, boy.' Fallen took hold of the bell chain and pulled on it. Both lawmen could hear a bell ringing inside the house.

The sound of footsteps came to their ears.

'Someone's coming, Marshal Fallen,' Elmer said. He rested an ear against the stout door. 'I can hear their footsteps.'

The words had barely left the deputy's mouth when the door opened and the light of countless lamps washed over them. A small female aged about forty looked out at them and nodded politely. By her black-and-white uniform it was obvious that this was a maid of some description.

'Howdy, ma'am.' Fallen nodded as he removed his hat.

'And to what do we owe this honour, Marshal?' she asked.

Fallen smiled and held his Stetson across his midriff with his large hands. 'Is the judge at home?'

The maid looked surprised by the question.

'No, I'm afraid not,' she answered. 'Judge Silver never comes back here on poker nights. He plays cards with his friends and usually arrives back in the early hours.'

Fallen rubbed his jaw. 'You mean he's still back in town, ma'am?'

She nodded. 'That's right. On poker nights he finishes work and then has something to eat and then proceeds to the Diamond Pin hotel. The judge is a creature of habit. He never deviates from his regular routine on poker nights. Is something wrong? You look troubled, Marshal.'

'I just wanted to have a word with him,' Fallen bluffed. 'There's nothing wrong.'

Elmer moved closer to the marshal.

'We must have passed him on the way here,' he whispered. 'I'll bet he was in one of the cafés that we rode past to get here, Marshal Fallen.'

Not wishing to alarm the maid, Matt Fallen pushed his deputy away and gave a courteous bow to the woman. 'Thank you kindly, ma'am. Reckon we'd best be going.'

The pathway was suddenly enveloped in shadows as the maid closed the door behind the pair of lawmen. Fallen guided Elmer back to where they had left the horses. He placed his hat back on his head and bit his lower lip thoughtfully.

'C'mon, Elmer,' Fallen urged his deputy. 'We ain't got no time to waste if we intend getting to the judge before that killer does.'

'We already wasted a heap of time

getting these nags and riding them all the way out here, Marshal Fallen,' Elmer said. He pulled his reins free of the tree branch and reached up for his saddle horn. 'It'll be just our luck, nothin' else, if Judge Silver don't get his brains blowed out before we can get back to warn him.'

Fallen stepped into his stirrup and hauled his large frame on to his saddle. He gathered up his leathers and turned the horse away from the house. He knew that every word his deputy had uttered was correct but was uneasy at the younger man's attitude.

'Do you know what a pessimist is, Elmer?' he asked his deputy as the youngster turned his mount.

'A what?' Elmer frowned as he considered the unfamiliar word. 'Nope. I ain't ever heard of one of them critters. What in tarnation is it?'

'I'll buy you a mirror tomorrow, Elmer,' Fallen said and smiled. He tapped his heels and got the horse moving. 'Then you'll get a good look at one.'

The deputy in hot pursuit of the marshal, the pair of lawmen galloped back along the dusty road towards the heart of the sprawling settlement.

There was urgency in their spurs.

5

Lantern-light spilled out from the hardware store window and cast its amber glow over the elderly doctor and the remains of Seth Gordon. Doc Weaver eased his arthritic bones up until he was standing, then removed his battered derby and dried his brow with a handkerchief from his coat pocket. He was getting used to being called away from his whiskey bottle to tend dead men with small bullet holes in their chests.

It was becoming a habit. One he did not care for.

Doc replaced his derby and pushed the handkerchief back into his pocket as he pondered over the body at his feet. He had seen many killings over the years but none that could match this evening's toll.

The three men had been killed in a brutal, heartless fashion. Shot with uncanny accuracy and then left as though they were little more than smouldering cigar butts.

Doc screwed up his wrinkled eyes and stared down at Gordon's body. He shook his head as he tried vainly to understand such cold-hearted slaughter.

He sighed and shrugged. He had done his job and pronounced the attorney dead. The town owed him another two dollars to add to the other four he had already earned since sundown. The sound of the undertaker's black vehicle caught his attention as it pulled up beside the boardwalk. He stood aside on his ancient legs and allowed the undertaker and his assistant to get down from their high perch and lift Seth Gordon's limp body off the ground. Doc watched silently as the men carefully placed it in the back of the hearse.

Doc touched his hat brim to the older of the two men.

'Sam,' he muttered gruffly as he shuffled his footwear.

'We've both made us a tidy sum tonight, Doc,' undertaker Sam Smith said from behind a wide grin. He rubbed his hands together gleefully. 'I've never had so much business in one night.'

Doc raised a bushy eyebrow and nodded. He found his pipe and placed it in his mouth. 'Sure has been busy and no mistake, Sam.'

As his young helper closed the rear door of the hearse and climbed up behind the pair of matched black geldings, the undertaker leaned in closer to his old pal.

'Where the hell is Marshal Fallen anyway, Doc?' he asked. He pulled out his gold watch from his vest and flicked open its lid. 'He's usually here whenever a body is found. This ain't no time for him to go getting himself lost.'

Doc leaned over and checked the time from his friend's watch. 'Matt and Elmer rode off someplace a while back. Reckon they didn't expect another body to turn up so soon after the first two.'

Smith clapped his hands together.

'I ain't grumbling. I'm running out of places to lay them dead 'uns out, Doc,' Sam said, climbing up the side of the hearse beside his assistant. 'My funeral parlour is getting real crowded. Me and Orin here will have to start boxing them up before that killer strikes again.'

'Reckon so.' Doc nodded and ignited a match on his pants leg. He watched as the hearse slowly rolled away, heading back to the undertaker's parlour.

The medical man picked up his black bag and, with smoke billowing from his pipe bowl, he watched as the crowd slowly dispersed.

Doc scratched his whiskers thoughtfully.

'I wonder where Matt and Elmer went?' he asked himself, chewing on the pipe stem. 'They should have bin here. Matt got no call to go riding off like that.'

Doc ambled back in the direction of his office as buggies passed his weary shoulders. He squinted at the finery on display and took a puff with every step. He paused for a moment and watched as the street outside the Tivoli started fill with vehicles.

'Looks like the Tivoli has opened its doors,' he muttered, continuing on his way along Front Street. 'Damned if they'll get me in there.'

His ancient eyes observed men escorting their well-dressed female companions from the buggies and making their way to the brightly illuminated Tivoli. He chuckled to himself as he thought about the place they were entering. Six months earlier none of the men would have even considered taking their females into the unrefurbished saloon.

Now it was considered a theatre and that was OK.

Doc took another ten steps, then stopped. He tilted his head and looked out from under the brim of his hat at the Longhorn saloon opposite. The far less ornate saloon had none of the elegance of its near neighbour but it had the one thing Doc craved to wash the taste of death from his old throat. A wry smile stretched his wrinkled face as he stepped along the boardwalk and headed towards the drinking hole.

The scent of stale tobacco smoke and even staler alcohol filled Doc's flared nostrils as he approached the batwings and raised his free hand.

Doc pushed the swing doors apart and entered.

The man behind the bar counter touched his temple in silent greeting to one of his most regular patrons.

'Whiskey,' Doc called out to the bartender as he hurried between the other customers towards the mahogany counter. The elderly man placed his bag on the counter and winked at the bartender. 'Make it a double.'

6

Blazing torches sent billowing smoke down through the wide streets of War Smoke from outside the newly refurbished Tivoli saloon. The flames that leapt from the coal-tar poles set to either side of the large saloon illuminated half the street as carriages of every description brought people from the surrounding settlements to enjoy the Tivoli's latest innovation.

For years the Tivoli had been nothing more than another drinking hole, exactly like the dozen or more others scattered around War Smoke. Now it had been totally rebuilt so that it was no longer just a saloon.

It was also a fully equipped theatre.

A working stage had been constructed at the opposite end of the saloon's long bar counter. Upon this stage high calibre entertainment was about to be lavished upon the Tivoli's patrons.

The stage had operational velvet drapes as well as boxes at the sides from which the better quality of guests could look down upon the poorer members of the audience. Twenty mirrored lamps set around the rim of the raised stage would enhance the performers and amaze as well as mystify most members of the audience.

A few of the town's dignitaries had been given free tickets to attend the grand opening and most of them were in the audience. It seemed that only Marshal Fallen and his deputy had not put on their Sunday best and joined the rest of the people who were crowding into the Tivoli.

There were also three other missing faces. Seth Gordon, Lou Franklin and Holt Berkley had unexpected appointments with the Grim Reaper.

There was a sense of anticipation in the air. For months Willard Parker, the owner of the Tivoli, had promised that for the first time in this part of the West the audience would be treated to a show none of them would ever forget.

Parker had had 2,000 flyers printed and sent out to every ranch and town within ten miles of War Smoke. The message promised entertainment such as you might expect in one of the best theatres back East.

A string of top acts had been lured from the relative safety and comfort of their usual haunts and paid top dollar to travel to the Tivoli to perform.

Contrary to what most of the Easterners believed, it was usually far safer in the West than in the densely populated cities on the Eastern seaboard.

Until tonight.

A wealthy businessman after years of speculation in various money-making enterprises, Willard Parker believed that this was the time to introduce a spot of culture to War Smoke and make a fortune from those who normally had little upon which to spend their wealth.

By the look of it, Parker had been correct.

The street outside the saloon was full of buggies and a variety of other vehicles. There was still an hour to go before the curtain went up on his grand reopening of the Tivoli, and already the place was was nearly full.

Parker rested his shoulder against the wall and nodded politely to every man and woman who passed by him to pay their money at the newly erected box-office.

A man clad in the finery of a riverboat gambler ambled up beside Parker and smiled. Drew Clancy was known throughout the territory for his skill as a poker player and his deadly accuracy with the array of weaponry he always had secreted around his body. Clancy had killed ten people since his arrival in War Smoke, yet he had never spent any time in jail. Every one of the killings had been within the law, for he had never drawn first.

He scratched a match and touched the end of a long thin cigar as it rested between his teeth. He inhaled the smoke and then looked at Parker.

'You should have the sign repainted after this, Will,' he advised through a line of tobacco smoke.

Parker glanced at Drew.

'Why would I have the sign repainted, Clancy?' Parker asked while shaking another outstretched hand.

Drew whispered in Parker's ear. 'Replace the word 'saloon' with 'theatre', Will. That's what we've got here. A grand theatre.'

'I think you might be right.' Parker touched the brim of his top hat. 'Theatre does sound better now that you mention it.'

'It sounds classy, Will.' Drew smiled and gave a fleeting glance at the box office. 'You've created something big here and I reckon it can only get bigger.'

Parker placed a hand on the gambler's shoulder. 'Let's go upstairs to my office, Clancy. We'll have a brandy before the show starts and discuss this matter further.'

Both men climbed the stairs to

Parker's private quarters. They entered the office and moved to a window which looked down upon the customers taking their seats in the theatre. From the window they could see the stage in all its splendour.

'How many of these acts are top notch, Will?' Clancy asked, having accepted the glass of fine cognac and inhaled its fumes.

Parker smiled. 'All of them, Clancy.'

The gambler shrugged and sat down in a chair facing the window. He swirled the brandy around in the glass and watched the stage and its closed drapes.

'You mean that you managed to lure the east coast's top entertainers all the way out here, Will?' he asked.

'My money did.' Parker smiled. He tapped ash from his cigar into a glass tray and took a seat next to his guest. 'I could have hired a handful of second-rate singers and dancers but I want this to work. I bought the best.'

Clancy nodded and took a sip of his drink. 'I think that you might have ensured the success of this operation, Will. Who have you got topping the bill?'

A broad smile crossed Parker's face.

'Have you ever heard of Mezmo the Great?' he asked.

Clancy leaned forward in his chair. 'You've got Mezmo?'

'Yep, I sure have, Clancy.' Parker sucked smoke into his lungs and then blew a line of it at the ceiling. 'I've got the greatest mesmerist that ever lived since Franz Anton Mesmer and he's working for me for the next week.'

Clancy shook his head in admiration. 'He must have cost you a fortune, Will. How in tarnation did you afford him?'

Parker looked through the smoke at his friend. There was a look of self-doubt in his face.

'You know something?' he said. 'I'm not sure. He wired me that as long as he could bring his new female assistant with him he would forgo his usual salary.'

'That doesn't make any sense!'

Clancy exclaimed. 'Mezmo working for nothing?'

Parker sat back in his chair. 'Don't look a gift horse in the mouth, Clancy. I'm sure he's got his reasons and I'm not dumb enough to ask too many questions. If he wants to work for nothing I'll let him.'

Drew Clancy stared down into the nearly full auditorium of the Tivoli, his mind racing. The gambler did not believe that anyone who was as famous as Mezmo would even consider travelling to a town most folks back East had never heard of and then be willing to work for nothing. Not even if it were to showcase his young protégée. Clancy rubbed his clean-shaven jaw and stared through the cigar smoke.

'I reckon you're right, but it sure sounds strange that someone like Mezmo the Great would come here and be willing to work without a fee.'

'He's richer than most,' Parker said. 'If this is the way he wants it then this is the way it's got to be. He'll draw in the crowds for the next week and establish the Tivoli as the best little theatre west of the Pecos, Clancy. Why should I fret?'

'Why indeed, Will.'

'Look at this.' Parker picked up a publicity portrait of his 'star' and handed it to the gambler. As Clancy stared at the picture of the great mesmerist he straightened up in his chair and suddenly realized who the picture reminded him of. A cold shiver traced along his spine. Even the greying hair and artistic licence could not hide the true identity of the famous Mezmo.

Clancy Drew placed the picture on the arm of his chair, held his hands before him as though in silent prayer and looked at his friend.

'Don't this Mezmo remind you of anybody, Will?' he asked the grinning Parker.

'No he don't, Clancy,' Parker answered. 'All Mezmo reminds me of is money. The money he's gonna make me over the next week by performing on my

Tivoli stage. Him working for free is a bonus, Clancy.'

'You might be right but I've got me a gut feeling that there's more to this Mezmo than meets the eye, Will,' Clancy said as doubts crowded into his mind.

Parker pointed at the gambler.

'I'm just lucky, Clancy.' He smirked. 'I always have been.'

Drew Clancy set his brandy down and stood, rising to his full height. To the surprise of his host the gambler moved towards the staircase. Before leaving his host, Clancy turned and looked at Parker.

'There's two kinds of luck, Will,' he muttered. 'There's good luck and there's bad luck. Sometimes one can come disguised as the other.'

The owner of the Tivoli raised his eyebrows and sipped his brandy. Then he gave a shrug. He watched Clancy as the lean gambler made his way down the stairs. Parker did not know what the gambler meant, but he did not truly care.

He roared with laughter.

'Sour grapes, Clancy.' Parker grinned into the fragrant fumes of his brandy and looked down into his packed saloon. There was barely an empty seat. 'You could have invested in this enterprise, but like everybody else in War Smoke you figured it was nothing but a folly. My folly.'

7

The name of Mezmo was one that Drew Clancy had heard of but it was the likeness of the features that had chilled his soul. The gambler had seen that face before and it troubled him as he vainly tried to remember where and when. All Clancy knew for sure was that it was a face of a man he had long thought dead. The gambler moved swiftly to the back of the stage area, determined to see that face close up. Clancy wanted to find out whether he was right or wrong in being so concerned.

He moved quickly through the well-concealed utility area which led directly to the rear of the Tivoli. He sidestepped the numerous stagehands and dancers as they went about their well-rehearsed jobs in readiness for the opening act.

The backstage area of the Tivoli was like a rabbit warren but the gambler seemed to know exactly where he was going as he moved past the dozens of people to where his keen eyesight had spotted the name scrawled upon the paper star pinned to one of the dressing-room doors. He strode up to the door and without a moment's hesitation knocked on its freshly painted surface.

'You in there, Mezmo?' he called, raising his voice.

Other performers glanced along the line of dressing-rooms at the gambler, but in a very few seconds they had all lost interest and resumed what they had been doing.

'Open this damn door. I wanna talk with you,' Clancy shouted again.

Almost instantly the door was unlocked and opened.

The two men stared into one another's eyes. The man who called himself Mezmo the Great looked deeply into the eyes of Clancy and then slowly smiled. All of a sudden Clancy felt light-headed and slightly confused.

'What can I do for you, young man?' the silver-haired Mezmo asked. 'Why did you summon me to this door?'

Clancy stared hard at the face. For a brief moment he thought that he recognized the strange figure, but then he was not so certain. The greasepaint disguised most of the mesmerist's features for close inspection. The gambler ran his fingers through his hair and tilted his head.

'Are you Mezmo?' he asked. He was starting to doubt his own eyes. 'Mezmo the Great?'

'Indeed I am,' Mezmo replied in a darkly charming tone. 'Why do you ask?'

Drew Clancy had no idea why he was questioning the famed Mezmo. He pulled the cigar from his lips and took a step backwards as his numbed mind tried to remember.

'I'm s-sorry,' he stammered. 'I thought that we'd met once but now I'm not so sure.'

Mezmo nodded his head slowly. 'Yes, my friend. You were wrong. Now if you will excuse me I have to finish my make-up.'

'I'm sorry.' Clancy forced a smile and turned away.

The sound of the dressing-room door being closed behind him filled the gambler with even more uncertainty. He blinked hard, plucked the cigar from his lips and stared at it. He cast a brief glance over his shoulder, then started to retrace his steps. With every stride of his long legs the dark tones of the mesmerist filled his mind.

Clancy passed through a side door into the auditorium and walked slowly around the audience who were waiting in excited anticipation for the show to begin. The gambler reached the bar counter without even knowing how he had got there. He touched his temple. He felt as though his brain had been frozen inside his skull.

Clancy tossed a silver dollar on to the counter and signalled the bartender for three fingers of whiskey. The bartender was an obliging character and placed a small thimble glass between the gambler's hands.

The whiskey was poured from the clear glass bottle and quickly filled the glass.

As soon as the glass was filled, Clancy tossed the fiery liquor down his throat and indicated for the action to be repeated.

Again the bartender obliged. Clancy looked over his shoulder at the expectant crowd. He downed the whiskey in one swift throw and tried to remember everything he had been going to say to the great Mezmo. No matter how hard he tried, Clancy could not recall why he had marched to the dressing room or what he intended saying to the mysterious man.

His mind was confused.

It was as though the famed mesmerist had washed his mind clean of everything. Every one of his thoughts had just disappeared.

Clancy pointed at the glass a third time.

His eyes narrowed as he placed the cigar in a glass ashtray and pulled another silver coin from his vest pocket.

'Same again,' Clancy said to the bartender. He placed the dollar on the counter.

'You look like you seen a ghost, Clancy,' the bartender said, pouring the amber liquor into the small glass. 'I've never seen you look so spooked before.'

Drew Clancy picked up the glass and poured the whiskey down his throat. He placed the glass down and nodded at the man with the bottle in his hand.

'Funny you should say that, Jim.' He sighed as the bartender refilled the glass. 'That's just the way I feel. I'm like a man who has just seen a ghost and is real spooked.'

'What happened, Clancy?' the bartender asked.

Drew Clancy shrugged and then shook nervously. 'Damned if I know, Jim. Damned if I know.'

★   ★   ★

The great Mezmo was seated in front of the mirror, applying the last touches of greasepaint to his features. It was a ritual he had mastered long ago to disguise his features. He had not spoken since closing the dressing-room door. Now, as he patted the small make-up sponge over his neck, he smiled.

'Who was that, Mezmo?' a beautiful young female asked from the depths of a soft chair. 'You seemed to recognize that man by the tone in your voice.'

'You're learning, Victoria.' Mezmo smiled at her and continued to apply the finishing touches to his greasepaint mask.

'You didn't answer me, Mezmo,' she said.

'Didn't I?' Mezmo paused and turned his head to look at her fondly.

'You know you didn't, Mezmo.' Victoria Vale was the most stunning female on the bill. She was also as mysterious as the man who employed her. Nobody apart from Mezmo knew anything about her. It was thought he had actually created her out of thin air a year earlier, for no records were known to exist concerning the beautiful young woman. She had no date of birth. No family. Nothing, apart from the day she had first appeared on stage with the great Mezmo, was known to the outside world.

Before that time Victoria Vale had

apparently never existed.

'Answer my question, Mezmo,' she pressed. 'Who was that fancy dude you just put a spell on?'

'That, my dear Victoria, was one of the reasons we came all the way here to perform.' The mesmerist smiled and then returned his attention to the mirror. 'Drew Clancy does not remember because I have wiped his memory clean. He shall not remember a thing until I allow him to do so.'

'I don't understand,' Victoria said. She moved over to sit on the couch in the dressing-room. 'What has that man got to do with our coming to War Smoke?'

The great Mezmo smiled as he darkened his eyelashes with a well-worn make-up stick.

'It was a long time ago, my dear,' he replied. 'Probably before you were even conceived. He and some of his friends did something illegal.'

'Why should that be of interest to you?' Victoria sat upright on the couch. She stared at her small feet.

'No reason, my dear,' Mezmo lied. 'No reason at all.'

She stood up and stared at the seated man. 'Don't talk in riddles. How can he have something to do with us coming here and then not have anything to do with it? How?'

'We make our living by creating riddles, Victoria,' Mezumo told her drily. 'I thought you knew that? Nothing is real and nothing is impossible. I could lasso the moon if I wanted to do so. Or maybe I would just make the audience believe I'd lassoed the moon. Everything is an illusion.'

The spirited young woman squared up to the great mesmerist and wagged a finger at him. 'Sometimes you really anger me. It's like you don't trust me. Hell, I don't even know when I'm on stage performing. I blink and you tell me the show's over.'

Mezmo turned on his chair and looked up at her. Their eyes met and he smiled. He stood and kept looking into her eyes as his fingers ran down the side of her face.

'You feel tired, Victoria,' he whispered. 'You'd better have a nap before the show starts.'

She was about to protest, but then she yawned and touched her brow. She flopped back on to the couch and rested her head on a cushion.

'I'm tired, Mezmo,' she murmured. She sighed heavily, her lashes fluttered and her eyes closed. 'I'll just take a short nap before the show starts.'

'You do that, Victoria.' He smiled and nodded. 'You rest for a little while.'

She was virtually unconscious within seconds of shutting her eyes and the famed expert mesmerizer knew she would remain that way until he returned. He picked up a black hat with a wide floppy brim and placed it over his silver hair.

The sounds of the other performers outside his dressing-room filled his ears. He knew that from now on the back-stage area would be organized chaos. It would not return to normality until the last curtain call.

Mezmo then heard the opening

music wafting through to the backstage area of the Tivoli. The show was about to begin. Being top of the bill, Mezmo knew exactly how long it would be before he and Victoria were due on stage. He checked his pocket watch and nodded to himself.

There was plenty of time, he thought. He slid the watch back into his pocket and crossed the room.

He plucked a large black hooded coat off a stand and draped it over his shoulders. He then opened the door of the dressing-room, paused and glanced back at his beautiful assistant.

'Sleep, my beautiful waif,' he commanded quietly. 'Sleep until I return.'

8

With Front Street full to overflowing with every kind of horse-drawn conveyance filling its width, Matt Fallen pulled back on his reins and stopped his mount a hundred yards away from the hitching rail outside his office. For a moment the lawman wondered what was going on, then he saw the constant flow of people heading into the Tivoli. He jerked the long leathers to his right and steered the horse to the hitching pole outside the Longhorn. The high-shouldered animal stopped before the saloon's water trough, dropped its head and started drinking.

Fallen swung one long leg over his cantle and dismounted just as his deputy rode up behind him. The marshal exhaled and tossed his long leathers up into Elmer's hands.

'Take these nags back to the livery,

Elmer,' he said. He squinted up and down the long thoroughfare. 'Then come running back here. Reckon we'll do our rounds of the town then.'

'Can we get us some supper before we do the rounds, Marshal Fallen?' Elmer asked. 'I'm powerful hungry.'

'We'll eat when I say so,' the marshal growled. 'First things first.'

'What you gonna do, Marshal Fallen?' the deputy asked, steadying the lathered-up horse beneath him.

Fallen shook his head. 'I'll be having myself a drink. A drink of whiskey to wash the trail dust out of my throat. Then I'm gonna try and figure out where the judge is.'

Elmer cupped his ear and looked towards the brightly illuminated refurbished saloon. 'Reckon the show up at the Tivoli has done started already, Marshal. Judge Silver might have gone there when he found out two of his pals are dead.'

'Three,' Doc corrected. He was standing beside the Longhorn's swing doors and studying his pals. 'There was another killing after you boys rode out.'

'Another killing?' Elmer gasped.

'Who got themselves killed, Doc?' Fallen stepped up on to the boardwalk and stood beside his old friend.

'Seth Gordon, Matt,' Doc replied. He stroked his whiskers. 'Shot through the heart with a small-calibre gun just like the other two.'

'Seth's dead?' In consternation Fallen repeated the name. 'Damn it all. Me and Elmer rode to warn the judge and Gordon was the next target.'

'Did you warn the judge, Matt?' Doc wondered.

'We did not.' Elmer shook his head. 'The judge weren't even there. His woman said he's still in town some-place. She reckoned he ain't due home until the early hours.'

'His maid,' Fallen corrected. 'The maid told us he was still in War Smoke, Doc.'

Elmer frowned. 'Ain't that what I just said?'

Doc chewed his lip thoughtfully as he

looked at the marshal.

'You owe me another two dollars,' he said.

'You'll get it, Doc,' Fallen told him. 'I don't suppose there were any witnesses to give us a clue as to what our killer looks like, were there?'

'Not a one, Matt.' Doc sniffed the air. 'It's like that killer just appears and vanishes at will. Damn spooky if you ask me.'

Elmer leaned from his mount. 'I told you it was a ghost, Doc. Didn't I say that? We ain't dealing with a real living person here. This has all the hallmarks of being done by a varmint from the other side. Mark my words. We've locked horns with a ghost.'

'A ghost with a six-shooter?' Fallen stared at his deputy in disbelief. 'Well he's sure gonna be hard to kill, Elmer. Him being dead already, I mean.'

Elmer raised his eyebrows. 'Ain't that a puzzlement?'

'Take them horses back to the livery, boy,' Fallen growled and pointed in the direction of the stables. 'Now.'

As the muttering deputy rode away with the marshal's horse in tow the old doctor led Fallen into the Longhorn.

'I know it sounds loco, Matt,' he said. 'But Elmer's got a point. This does seem like the work of some supernatural critter.'

'Don't tell me you believe in all that trash as well, Doc,' the lawman said, sighing. 'Elmer fills his head with all sorts of dime-novel stories and believes them all.'

'I don't read dime novels, Matt,' Doc said. 'I just said it seemed like this killer strikes and vanishes real fast. A weak mind could be fooled into thinking it was something supernatural, though.'

Matt Fallen was smiling as they reached the bar counter.

'Don't be feared, Doc,' he said. He rested his large hands on the damp surface of the bar. 'This is the work of a living man. Mark my words, the killer ain't no ghost. That's the only thing I'm certain about.'

Two whiskeys were placed before the two men.

Fallen pulled a coin from his vest and flicked it into the bartender's hands. He pushed his hat off his brow and shook his head, trying to fight off his weariness.

'This is plumb loco, Doc,' the marshal growled. He picked up the glass and sipped at its fiery contents. 'Who wants them men dead and why?'

Doc lifted his glass and squinted at its contents.

'It seems to me that it has to be someone from out of town, Matt,' he reasoned.

'How can you be so sure?' Fallen yawned, then finished his drink. 'There are plenty of gun-toting critters in War Smoke capable of killing that same way, Doc.'

Doc raised an eyebrow. 'But the killings only started tonight, Matt. Think about it. Them strangers in town only arrived in the last couple of days.'

Fallen inhaled deeply. 'You're talking

about them folks that Will Parker hired and brought to War Smoke, ain't you?'

'Yep,' Doc nodded, 'anyone else in town could have killed Holt and the others any time they liked.'

Matt Fallen rose, stretching his huge frame, as Elmer entered the saloon and wandered up to them.

'Where'd we put them free passes for tonight's show at the Tivoli, Elmer?' the lawman asked.

Elmer grinned and fished around in his britches pocket until he produced the tickets.

'Right here, Marshal Fallen.' He smiled and waved the tickets under the marshal's nose.

Fallen nodded.

'C'mon, boy. We're going to the show,' he said.

'But I ain't had me drink yet, Marshal Fallen,' Elmer meekly protested. 'My throat's as dry as an eagle vulture's nest.'

'A young virile buck like you don't need liquor to fuel his cravings, Elmer,'

Fallen told him. He grabbed the deputy and turned him back towards the swing doors. 'Besides, it'll only stunt your growth.'

Doc sipped at his drink as the two lawmen marched out into the street and set off for the Tivoli. With wrinkled eyes he looked at the bartender.

'Don't go fretting, my sorrowful friend. I'll not leave you,' he joked. 'Not until the shooting starts again, any-ways.'

9

The smell of steaming horses filled the street as Matt Fallen and Elmer battled through the abandoned buggies in an attempt to reach their office. Eventually the lawmen reached the opposite board-walk and strode beneath the porch overhangs until they reached the mar-shal's office. Fallen unlocked the door and entered, his deputy hot on his heels.

'It sure is dark in here, Marshal Fallen,' Elmer said. He checked the stove. 'At least the stove is still lit.'

The marshal struck a match, touched the wick of the lamp on his desk, then lowered the glass funnel over the little flame. He adjusted the lamp's wheel until the office was bathed in light.

'That's better,' he said.

Elmer stared out at the horses and buggies crowding the thorougfare. 'There sure are a heap of vehicles blocking

Front Street, Marshal Fallen.'

'Hell, we know where the owners are, don't we?' Fallen picked up a key and tossed it into the deputy's hands.

'What's this for?' Elmer asked.

Fallen pointed at the rifle rack attached to the wall beside the door leading to the jail cells.

'Get yourself a rifle, Elmer,' he ordered his deputy. 'And make sure it's loaded.'

The deputy pushed the key into a padlock and released the long chain which was threaded through the various weapons' trigger guards.

'What kinda rifle do you want, Marshal Fallen?' Elmer asked.

'I don't want one.' Fallen looked at his unarmed deputy. 'Get yourself a rifle, boy. You're the one who needs a gun, not me.'

Elmer scratched his whiskerless chin thoughtfully and studied the rifles. 'Should I get me a Winchester? I ain't never fired a repeating rifle.'

'And you ain't starting now.' Fallen shook his head. 'Get yourself a scattergun and fill your pockets with shotgun shells.'

As the deputy obeyed the lawman and pulled a shotgun off the rack, Fallen set about opening and closing drawers in his desk.

'What you looking for, Marshal Fallen?' the deputy asked. Carefully he placed a shotgun on to the desk and rethreaded the chain through the rifles.

'We come here to get you armed and for me to check something out,' Fallen answered. 'I'm looking for old Wanted posters.'

The deputy secured the padlock and placed the key on the ink blotter. 'I don't see why I need a shotgun for. I got me a real handy .45 at my ma's place.'

Fallen paused and looked at Elmer. 'It ain't very handy if it's at her house, is it? You're meant to wear that gun all the time, Elmer. How come you keep forgetting to put the damn thing on?'

The deputy shrugged. 'It's real heavy.'

The tall lawman pointed at the tin stars pinned on their vests. 'There are a lot of folks out there that see these stars and use them for target practice, Elmer. I'd like to think that you'd be able to shoot back if they do.'

'But the belt is too big, Marshal Fallen,' Elmer grumbled. He wandered across the office to the stove, opened its door and peered inside. 'It keeps slipping off my hips with the weight of my .45.'

The marshal shook his head. 'Then get your ma to take it in for you so it won't end up around your ankles.'

Elmer grinned and pushed two shells into the hefty shotgun. 'Should I feed the stove, Marshal Fallen? It's getting colder.'

'Good idea. Put a couple of logs in it,' the marshal said. He sighed. 'I got me a feeling we'll be up all night chasing this killer. Best keep that stove fed, boy.'

Elmer pushed a couple of logs into the potbellied stove's glowing heart and carefully closed its iron door. He picked up the coffee pot from the stove's flat top.

'We still got us plenty of coffee left in this pot, Marshal,' Elmer observed with a grin and he filled a tin cup with the stewed beverage. 'You want a cup?'

'That coffee's half a day old, Elmer,' the marshal said. 'It ain't like fine wine. It don't improve with age, you know.'

Elmer took a sip of coffee and smiled. 'It tastes just fine to me, Marshal Fallen. You sure you don't want a cup?'

'I'm sure.' Fallen rubbed a knuckle across his brow.

'Tell me something, Marshal,' Elmer said, nursing the hot cup in his hands. 'Do you reckon we're gonna catch this murderous critter before he kills again?'

Fallen did not have a clear-cut answer for Elmer. All he had was a hunch gnawing at his craw. Something buried deep in the darkest recess of his memory was nagging at the seasoned lawman. Yet no matter how hard he tried to recall the all but forgotten episode, he could not pin down what it was that kept trying to rise up from the graveyard of his subconscious.

The marshal picked up a pile of Wanted posters that he'd taken from one of his desk drawers. He dropped it on top of his already cluttered desk and started going through the leaflets one by one.

Elmer ambled up beside the marshal with the tin cup still in his hands. He tilted his head and gave a pained expression.

'You ain't gonna learn much from them old circulars, Marshal Fallen,' he said, sipping the strong coffee. 'Them posters gotta be at least five years old. Maybe even older. What do you figure you're likely to find out by looking at them?'

'Maybe nothing, boy.' Matt Fallen glanced briefly at his deputy. 'It ain't gonna hurt if I take me a quick look, though.'

'Why don't you look at the new circulars instead of them old 'uns?'

Elmer wondered. 'Most of those are out of date. I bet half the killers on them are already dead.'

'I know that, Elmer.' Fallen nodded but he kept turning the posters over and studying them. 'Something's telling me that the critter I'm looking for might be on one of these old posters, though. Since Holt Berkley was gunned down I've had this notion burning in my guts.'

'That's just hunger, Marshal Fallen.' Elmer grinned and placed his cup next to the coffee pot. 'You're plumb starving like I am. We should go to one of the eating places and have us a steak or something.'

'I think you've got something there, boy.' Now Fallen looked up from the posters he had been studying.

Elmer looked at Fallen. 'We gonna go get us a couple of steaks?'

'Hell no!' the tall lawman said, stretching up to his full height. 'You mentioned food. I forgot that the housekeeper at the judge's house said Silver would go get himself some grub after he finished work and before he went to his poker game.'

Elmer stared blankly at his superior. 'What's that gotta do with us getting some vittles, Marshal Fallen?'

Fallen walked round the desk and thrust the shotgun into Elmer's hands. 'You're smarter than you look, Elmer. Judge Silver might still be eating. If we can find him before he heads on down to the Red Dog, we might be able to stop him getting shot.'

The deputy exhaled. 'If we find him can we have us something to eat? I'm powerful hungry.'

The marshal pushed a box of shotgun cartridges into his deputy's hands and opened the office door again. He paused on the boardwalk, glanced along Front Street, then pointed to the corner of Baker Street.

'The courthouse is down yonder,' Fallen said. Elmer locked the office door and staggered to his side with the hefty rifle and box of shells in his hands. 'All we gotta do is find the closest café to the courthouse. With any luck, the judge will still be in there, eating.'

'Lucky old judge.' Elmer sniffed.

Fallen strode off in the direction of the courthouse with Elmer in close pursuit. The youngster managed to empty the cartridges into his shirt pocket and discard the box before either of them reached the corner. He rested the twin-barrelled weapon on his bony shoulder and hurried his steps to catch up with the lawman.

'We still don't know for sure that Judge Silver is gonna be the killer's next victim, Marshal,' Elmer said as they turned the corner into Baker Street. 'For all we know that gun-happy madman is just murdering folks for the sheer hell of it.'

After ten strides Matt Fallen stopped and pointed at two of the town's best eating places. He then looked at a building a few hundred yards away. The courthouse was in darkness but a solitary street-lantern cast its eerie light across its façade.

'By my reckoning Rose's Café is closest to the courthouse, Elmer,' The lawman drawled. 'Judge Silver is a tad rotund and I don't reckon he'd walk too far to get himself a meal.'

'He is fat, Marshal Fallen,' Elmer agreed with a sigh. 'And I'm getting even hungrier with the smell of all that grub wafting over us.'

Fallen quickened his pace and ran towards the café with his deputy on his heels. The two lawmen jumped up on to its boardwalk and swiftly went inside.

The marshal's gaze darted across the faces of the customers, searching for the judge. Buxom Rose O'Hara, the owner of the café, moved between the tables and chairs towards them.

'What are you looking for, Matt?' she asked with a gleam in her eye.

'Has Judge Silver bin in here tonight, Rose?' Fallen asked the curvaceous female.

She smiled. 'He sure has. That man sure can eat up a storm. He had himself an inch-thick steak with fried potatoes followed up by a whole apple pie.'

The hungry Elmer peered around his superior's shoulder. 'He had himself a whole apple pie, Marshal Fallen.'

Fallen moved closer to Rose O'Hara.

'How long since he left, Rose?' he asked. She glanced up at the wall clock.

'No more than five minutes ago by my reckoning,' she replied. 'Is something wrong, Matt?'

'I sure hope not,' Fallen answered. 'Which way did he go?'

'He cut up the lane, Matt,' Rose told him. 'It comes out beside the barber shop on Front Street. The judge said he was a tad late for his poker game.'

Fallen touched her cheek. 'Thank you kindly, Rose.'

Rose O'Hara watched as the pair of starpackers headed briskly for the door. She glanced at her customers and grinned at them.

'Matt Fallen moves fast for a big man, don't he?' she remarked, and chuckled.

The two lawmen raced along the boardwalk, jumped down on to the sandy street and ran up the dark lane. The high buildings were so close along each side that even starlight could scarcely penetrate to the footway.

The broad-shouldered Fallen ran along, carrying his unholstered gun. The gangly deputy followed less than a yard behind, toting the scattergun in his hands. The gloomy lane harboured eerie shadows all along its length.

'Can you see him yet, Marshal Fallen?' Elmer panted as his youthful legs tried to keep pace with the tall lawman.

'Not yet I can't, Elmer,' Fallen called back over his shoulder. 'He can't be far ahead of us, though. I can still smell his cigar smoke.'

Then, as they rounded a corner, a sharp, ear-splitting sound rent the air and a bright flash of light briefly lit up the lane, stopping both men in their tracks.

'Gunplay!' Fallen gasped.

'Oh, glory be!' Elmer clutched the marshal's arm. 'That shot came from up ahead.'

'I know that, boy,' Fallen said. He

pulled back on his gun hammer with his thumb until it locked into position. 'C'mon. There ain't no time to lose.'

The lawman knew that the solitary gunshot was an ominous forewarning. The killer they sought had yet to fire a second shot after his first had found its target.

They ran along the narrow lane towards where they had heard the shot ringing out, but now they ran faster. This time they did not intend to lose the mysterious killer in the shadows.

Fallen's muscular shoulders seemed to collide with every wall as he pounded along the narrow lane in pursuit of the deadly killer. The marshal did not want to find that another victim had been added to the killer's tally, but knew that the single gunshot made it almost inevitable.

As both the lawmen raced towards Front Street's lights they saw a large body lying crumpled on the ground in front of them them. The coal-tar lanterns illuminated the last twenty yards of the narrow lane, shedding their light over the grim sight, but it was not the dead man their narrowed eyes were staring at.

It was the figure that was moving hastily away.

'There he is, Elmer!' Fallen yelled as his deputy came breathlessly closer to the marshal's shoulder.

'I see the varmint, Marshal Fallen,' Elmer panted as he tried to lower the long barrels of the shotgun and aim it at the fleeing figure ahead of them.

The figure was clad all in black. His wide floppy hat brim made it impossible for either of his pursuers to identify who it was who fled from them. Both Fallen and Elmer could see the long caped coat stirring up dust as it flapped like the wings of some surreal creature.

'There he is, Marshal Fallen!' Elmer exclaimed, his thumbs feverishly clawing back on his weapon's hammers.

Not wanting to get between Elmer's charged scattergun barrels and the devilish killer, the marshal moved aside from his deputy.

'Stop!' Fallen shouted loudly. He aimed his six-shooter at the running figure. 'Stop or I'll fire.'

The marshal's words did not stop the fleeing, black-draped figure. The apparition continued to run towards the brightly illuminated Front Street in his determination to reach the busy thoroughfare and disappear amongst the array of vehicles, horses and townsfolk.

Both Fallen and Elmer knew that the time for them to stop their prey was running out fast. If they were to end the slaughter, it had to be now.

'Shoot, Elmer!' Fallen yelled out above the sound of their pounding boot leather as reverberated off the high buildings.

Elmer pulled both triggers. A pair of snarling plumes of smoke blasted from the barrels of the shotgun. But the combination of movement and the weapon's violent kick were not a recipe for accuracy. A huge chunk of lumber was ripped out of one of the buildings above the fleeing figure.

Smouldering sawdust and chunks of splintered wood rained down into the lane as the lawmen kept running after their prey. As the exhausted deputy tried to pull fresh cartridges from his shirt pocket the rest of the shotgun shells fell on to the ground.

Fallen and Elmer were almost side by side. The marshal held his gun in his outstretched hand and aimed at the unholy vision ahead of them.

'Leave this to me, Elmer,' he said confidently. He closed one eye and desperately tried to get a bead on the figure, which had almost reached the end of the lane. Then he roared: 'Stop. I ain't gonna warn you again, fella.'

The long trailing black cape rose up and down like a bucking bronco. The killer had no intention of obeying the lawman's command.

True to his word the marshal squeezed on his trigger.

The deafening shot resounded along the narrow lane. It ripped through the figure's trailing cape and unbalanced the runner. The figure spun on his heels as the bullet nearly ripped the end off the billowing cape. Then, suddenly, the hunters and the hunted were facing each other. Without a second's hesitation the marshal's bullet was returned. The lane resounded as the small-calibre weapon spewed out its venom.

'Look out, Elmer,' the marshal yelled as he saw the bright eruption of lethal lightning heading toward them. The deputy came to an abrupt halt beside him.

Instinctively Matt Fallen ducked as the red-hot taper carved a path through the shadows and passed over his ducked head. The marshal was about to fire again when Elmer gave out an agonized groan. The sound of the bullet that had hit him rocked the walls on both sides.

As Fallen watched in horror the breached shotgun flew out of Elmer's hands. He clutched his chest and fell backwards into the gloom.

Elmer hit the ground hard.

Dust rose up from the ground around the felled deputy.

Fallen's eyes widened at the pitiful sight of his young friend on the ground. The stunned marshal looked down at the motionless deputy. Then he dropped to one knee.

'Elmer,' he stammered. His shaking hand reached out to the deputy as he stared helplessly at his young pal. The darkness in the lane could not conceal the truth from Fallen's eyes. He stared at the smoking bullet hole in the deputy's leather vest, close to the tin star. It was another perfectly placed shot. 'Speak to me, Elmer. You ain't dead, are you?'

There was no answer from the prostrate young lawman.

Fired by raging anger, Fallen narrowed his eyes, then pulled his gun hammer back. The sound of it clicking seemed unnaturally loud in the dark, narrow lane. He swung around and leapt up to his full height. He was about to squeeze his six-shooter's trigger when to his utter surprise he realized that the mysterious figure was gone.

'Damn!' he cursed.

The only thing in the lane besides the two lawmen and the lifeless banker was the lingering cloud of gunsmoke that hung in the air about four feet above the ground.

'You damn yella coward!' the marshal snarled.

Hastily, Matt Fallen released his gun hammer and then drove the Colt back into its holster. He mustered every scrap of his resolve, inhaled deeply and turned back to look down upon his deputy stretched out in the darkness. His seasoned eyes had seen more than their fair share of men cut down in their prime but none of those images compared to this.

'I'll kill that *hombre* for this,' he vowed.

Fallen dropped on to one knee and rested a hand on the shoulder of his deputy. Carefully he eased Elmer over until he was on his back. He looked down at the youngster and brushed the strands of limp hair off Elmer's face.

There was fire in the eyes of the lawman. He had not felt like this for a long while. The lawman was shaking as he squinted down at his trusted friend.

He had never felt quite so helpless.

'That cowardly *hombre* just made the biggest mistake of his life, Elmer boy,' Fallen whispered. He patted Elmer's shoulder gently. 'He killed my friend. He killed my best friend. That was a mistake he'll regret. Nobody kills my best friend and lives to brag about it.'

Suddenly the deputy started to shake. His eyes opened and glanced all around him before focusing on the started features of the marshal. Elmer winced and rubbed his chest.

'Who would that be, Marshal Fallen?' Elmer groaned. 'Who'd that varmint kill?'

The marshal's eyes widened in stunned awe as he stared at his deputy. He leaned forward and helped the youngster up into a sitting position.

'Elmer?' he gasped and ruffled the deputy's hair. 'You ain't dead.'

The dazed young deputy raised an eyebrow and looked at his boss curiously.

'I know I ain't dead.' Elmer clutched his throbbing skull and blinked hard. 'Who was you confabbing about a little while back, Marshal Fallen? You said that stinking critter killed your best friend. Who in tarnation was you talking about?'

Fallen helped his deputy up on to his feet and inspected him carefully. The bullet hole in the deputy's vest was in line with the youngster's heart. It made no sense to the tall lawman.

'How come you're still alive, Elmer?' he drawled. 'That *hombre* hit you dead centre. You oughta be dead.'

Elmer looked offended. 'Don't sound so miffed, Marshal. I figured I was dead too when I felt that bullet hit me in my chest. I'd have given odds that I was a goner and no mistake.'

Fallen grabbed a handful of the leather vest and poked his finger through the neat bullet hole in it. Then he spotted the thick wallet tucked into his deputy's shirt pocket. A wallet with a bullet stuck into its wad of banknotes.

'When did you get a wallet full of money, Elmer?' Fallen asked, easing it out of his deputy's shirt pocket. He studied it carefully. 'There must be at least two thousand dollars in here. Most of them got a bullet hole in them, though.'

Elmer rubbed his bruised chest. 'I forgot about that. Doc gave me that to give to you. It belongs to one of them card-playing men. Doc said he didn't want it falling into the hands of that skinny old undertaker.'

'You've had that wallet in your pocket all this time?' Fallen asked. Then he smiled. 'If I didn't know you so well I'd be thinking that maybe you was going to have yourself a fine ol' time with Maisie down at the Red Dog gambling hall.'

'I plumb forgot about it, Marshal Fallen.' Elmer shrugged innocently. 'What with all the goings-on around here tonight.'

'It's a good job you did forget about

it, Elmer.' The marshal pulled the small bullet out of the inch-thick stack of banknotes and held it up to the lantern-light. 'This little .22 would have killed you otherwise.'

The deputy rubbed his hand over his sweat-soaked face and gulped as Fallen forced the wallet into his pants pocket.

'Golly, Marshal Fallen. I could have ended up as dead as poor old Judge Silver here.'

Matt Fallen nodded and led his bruised deputy to the judge's body. He reached down, turned Jed Silver over on to his side and pulled his wallet out of his jacket's inside breast pocket. He opened the billfold and flicked the banknotes.

'The judge must have himself at least three thousand bucks here, Elmer. Reckon it was gonna be one hell of a poker game.'

Elmer held out his hand. 'Do you reckon I should look after it for you, Marshal Fallen?'

The lawman pushed his hat back until it rested on the crown of his head.

'Why would I want you to look after this billfold, Elmer?'

'Some ornery critter might try and kill me again,' Elmer said bluntly. 'These fat wallets sure can stop bullets.'

Fallen handed the wallet to his deputy. 'OK. You look after it, but mark my words, boy, it won't stop a .45-calibre bullet. We're lucky the killer has been using a .22.'

'I'd be dead otherwise.' Elmer gulped as he tucked the judge's wallet into his shirt pocket and patted it against his bruised chest. 'Why'd you reckon this killer is using such a little gun, Marshal Fallen? A .22 is usually a gal's gun.'

'Or a gambler's hidden weapon,' Fallen added. 'Or the weapon of choice to any *hombre* wanting to conceal his hardware from view.'

Elmer looked nervously around them. 'I don't rightly understand any of this, Marshal. At first you figure it must be a locobean killing all these folks, and then you ain't so sure. Seems to me like this *hombre* has got himself a plan.'

'I fear you're right, Elmer.' Fallen nodded in agreement and looked again at the lifeless body of Jed Silver. He patted the deputy's arm. 'C'mon. We'd best haul the judge down to the funeral parlour, boy.'

Elmer shook his head. 'We gotta get Doc to confirm that the judge is dead first, Marshal Fallen.'

'Hell! Even I can tell the judge is dead, Elmer.'

'That ain't the point.' Elmer frowned.

'You're right, Elmer.' The marshal smiled. 'I'd hate to deprive Doc of his two bucks. Go over to the Red Dog and drag him over here.'

The deputy plucked up the shotgun from the ground. He tilted his head and stared at the marshal.

'You never got round to telling me who you was talking about, Marshal Fallen,' he said. 'You know what I mean. You said that shadowy figure killed your best friend. Who exactly is your best friend?'

Fallen raised an eyebrow and cleared

his throat. 'Go and get Doc, Elmer.'

'But you ain't told me who you was talking about, Marshal Fallen.' Elmer rested the hefty double-barrelled weapon on his shoulder and kicked at the dust.

'I'll tell you later, boy.' Fallen put the wallet carefully into his inside vest pocket. 'Now go get Doc.'

10

The lavish interior of the Tivoli rocked with a mixture of every emotion known to man as its opening night gathered momentum. The cheering and applause could be heard halfway along Front Street as the culturally starved population of the frontier town finally began to relish the amazing stage acts they were witnessing.

Amid the hundreds of seated and standing members of the audience inside the Tivoli only one man had not succumbed to the variety of dancers, jugglers, knife-throwers and other entertainers.

Professional gambler Drew Clancy had leaned against the mahogany bar counter during the entire show and simply sipped his whiskey, as though he were deaf and blind to the entire spectacle.

Clancy did not know it but he was in a hypnotic trance and had been since he had confronted the strange figure calling himself Mezmo the Great. No amount of hard liquor seemed capable of snapping him out of the uncanny trance he had found himself in, but he kept sipping at his rye anyway.

'I can't figure how you're still standing, Mr Clancy,' the bartender said as he obeyed his customer's command and refilled the glass with whiskey for the umpteenth time. 'I've seen men buckle in a heap after drinking only half what you've downed.'

Clancy glanced at the bartender. 'Maybe old Willard is watering the whiskey. I sure don't feel drunk and I should be.'

'Is anything wrong?' The bartender looked concerned.

'I'm damned if I know,' Clancy replied. 'My head is hurting. I've had the weirdest pounding inside my skull for the last hour or so.'

The bartender glanced over the heads of the seated audience at the stage. The noise of the crowd grew louder as they clapped their hands together like performing sea lions. The gambler rubbed the nape of his neck and vainly attempted to unknot his neck muscles as they tightened. It was as though the entire building was vibrating with the continuous sound of all the acts and their musical accompaniment.

'How long does this go on?' Clancy asked the bartender.

'Too long.'

'I sure as hell pity you stuck here every night having to endure all this culture.' Clancy shook his head. 'I'd start shooting at them painted bastards just to make them hush up.'

Once again the bartender filled the gambler's glass with whiskey and scooped another gleaming coin into the palm of his hand.

'How come you ain't playing poker in one of the other saloons or gambling halls, Clancy?' the man asked, dropping the coin into the cash drawer behind him. 'What made you come here tonight? This sure ain't to your liking.'

The question burned into the poker player's head. Clancy picked up the small glass and stared at the amber contents as he tried to find an answer.

'You know something?' he muttered. 'I ain't got any idea why I came here. I can't even recall getting here.'

'This racket can't be helping your head,' the barman said as he polished glasses. 'If I had me a headache I'd be going someplace quiet and not hanging around here.'

Clancy knew the bartender was right but for some reason that he could not fathom, he felt compelled to stay. It was as if something inside his aching skull had been planted there without his knowledge and he was utterly helpless to fight against it.

He tossed the whiskey into his mouth. It barely touched the insides of his cheeks as it burned a trail down into his innards.

'Another whiskey, barkeep,' he said. His long slim fingers slid the glass towards the man with the bottle in his hand. 'I'm still thirsty and still trying to remember what in tarnation I'm doing in the one saloon in War Smoke that ain't got a poker game going.'

The bartender obliged and refilled the glass.

'By the time you get your memory back you'll be unconscious, Clancy,' he said, grinning.

Clancy almost smiled. 'I surely hope so.'

The unsuspecting Drew Clancy did not know it as he lifted the small glass to his lips but something had indeed been placed inside his mind. Although Clancy had no memory of it, he had encountered the mysterious Mezmo just after sundown. Since that brief encounter he had been nothing more than a puppet in the mesmerist's skilful hands. There was a stick of dynamite inside the gambler's mind and its fuse had already been lit.

The infamous poker player rubbed his throbbing temple and stared with ice-cold eyes at the bartender.

'Just keep the glass filled, *amigo*,' Clancy snarled.

'Anything you say, Clancy.' The frightened bartender nodded as he poured more liquid lightning into the small vessel. 'Anything you say.'

It was as though a volcanic eruption had just started to spit lava out into the heart of the Tivoli. Every single person in the audience sensed that the star of the show was about to make his long awaited entrance.

Two jugglers completed their ten-minute slot in the show by throwing knives from one side of the stage to the other. Startled onlookers watched in terrified awe as the two men, standing opposite one another, snatched the razor-sharp blades out of the air and returned them at unbelievable speed to each other. To the relief of the mixed crowd every blade was plucked out of the air without incident.

The two men, clad in colourful leotards, skipped to the footlights and bowed. The sense of expectation rose to even greater heights as the jugglers ran off the stage and disappeared into the shadows.

Men whistled. Females frantically clapped their hands together as a beautiful young dancer emerged from the left-hand side of the stage with a square piece of board in her hands. The board had just three words painted upon it.

Mezmo the Great.

The crowded saloon watched as the shapely young female walked from one side of the stage to the other so that everyone could read the sign. She gave a perky wink, then vanished between the long drapes.

Roaring applause filled the Tivoli as the main chandelier was lowered on a chain and its lights dimmed. The event that every one of the paying customers had waited so long for was about to begin.

The heart of the building went into a hush as the small group of musicians began playing the ominous introduction for the top of the bill.

As the expectancy grew for Mezmo the Great to make his appearance, Matt Fallen led Doc Weaver and Elmer into the Tivoli. Every seat in the saloon was occupied. Its aisles were filled with men pressed up against its walls. Every eye was on the darkened stage waiting to see the famed mesmerist suddenly appear.

Just like so many other famous performers, Mezmo would wait for the music to reach a climax. The audience had to be at fever pitch before he would step out and allow them to feast their eyes upon him.

Fallen walked to the bar and curled a finger at one of the bartenders. A large man with his midriff wrapped in a large white apron moved towards the trio.

'Howdy, Marshal,' he said, giving a big smile.

Doc and Elmer stood on either side of the tall lawman. Doc placed his black medical bag on the counter as Fallen tossed coins on to the highly polished mahogany.

'Three beers, barkeep,' Fallen drawled. His narrowed eyes surveyed the vast room and every person in it.

'What you looking for, Matt?' Doc asked as the wide-shouldered lawman continued to study the crowd.

'Just looking, Doc,' Fallen said as the three glasses of beer were placed before them. 'I've still got that feeling gnawing at my craw. The bastard we're hunting is in this building someplace and I intend finding him before he can kill anyone else.'

'How in tarnation are you holding up, Matt?' Doc asked, studying the tired marshal. 'You ain't slept in two days, boy.'

'I'll get plenty of sleep when I've finished that killer's spree, Doc,' Fallen replied. He continued to study the occupants of the large room. 'I got me a feeling he's in here someplace. If he is, I'll get him.'

Doc frowned. 'Just remember that this place is bursting at the seams with peaceful folks wanting to see a show,

141

Matt. You don't want any of them getting caught in the middle of a gunfight.'

Fallen nodded. 'I understand, Doc.'

Elmer sipped at his beer. 'Why can't we just enjoy this Mezmo critter, Marshal Fallen? I'm plumb tuckered out. My chest hurts.'

Doc patted the young deputy on the arm. He lifted his beer glass and took a mouthful of the beer. His expression changed as the amber liquid met his taste buds.

'At least Will Parker got some good beer in here at last.' He smiled. 'That stuff he used to sell weren't fit for washing your feet in.'

Elmer chuckled. 'You know something, Doc? You're real funny for an old-timer.'

Doc glanced up at Fallen. 'Drink your suds, Matt.'

Matt Fallen rubbed his eyes, smiled and turned to pick up his glass. Hardly had he taken a sip before he espied the unmistakable figure of the town's most notorious gambler propped up halfway along the bar.

'That's odd,' the lawman muttered, taking a mouthful of the beer. He stared from under his hat brim at Clancy.

'What's odd, Matt?' Doc asked, shuffling closer to the tall marshal. 'Who you looking at?'

Fallen lowered the glass and whispered out of the side of his mouth:

'Look down yonder, Doc. That's Drew Clancy, the poker player. What do you figure he's doing in here?'

'He sure ain't enjoying the show by the look on his face,' Doc surmised.

Elmer raised his eyebrows. 'It looks like he's just sipping on whiskey, Marshal Fallen. He's had two shots of rye since we stepped up to this here counter.'

'But why would a poker player like him waste his time in here?' Fallen wondered. His weary mind was trying to catch up with his gut instinct. 'There ain't no gambling going on in here tonight. Clancy's a professional poker player. Every minute he's standing at a bar, he's losing money.'

'Maybe he's just enjoying himself, Matt,' Doc suggested. He took another gulp of his beer. 'There are folks that do that, you know. They enjoy themselves. You might take a feather out of one of their caps and relax now and then.'

Never taking his eyes off the gambler, Fallen lowered his beer and wiped his mouth along his sleeve.

'He don't look like he's enjoying himself, Doc,' the marshal said. 'He's got an expression on him like someone who just had their face slapped.'

The deputy chuckled. 'He does look kinda sorrowful.'

'Three more beers, barkeep,' Fallen called. He lowered his empty glass and placed it next to the two empty vessels of his friends.

Doc adjusted his spectacles and rubbed his whiskers.

'Do you really figure that the killer that's bin terrorizing War Smoke is in here, Matt?' he asked.

Fallen nodded. 'Yep.'

Elmer looked all around them. 'There ain't nobody in here that looks anything like that evil critter we shared bullets with earlier, Marshal.'

Fallen looked at the three fresh glasses of beer before them. He glanced at the deputy with the bullet hole in his vest.

'You don't expect the killer to still be wearing that long black cape and floppy hat, do you?' he asked.

Doc nudged his tall companion and pointed his pipestem at the stage. His ancient eyes peered through his spectacles at the figure who was moving slowly from the shadows towards the footlights.

'You mean like him?'

'Golly!' Elmer gasped and rubbed the bullet hole in his vest. 'That sure looks like the varmint who shot at us, Marshal Fallen.'

Fallen was about to lift his glass when he too saw the blood-chillingly recognizable figure on the stage. He turned

145

and stared in disbelief at the unnerving sight of the mesmerist walking towards the footlights.

'He sure does, Elmer.'

The man in black had a large floppy hat concealing his features and wore his long black cape draped over his shoulders. Fallen straightened up to his full height and pushed his hat up off his brow.

'What the hell?' he cursed.

Elmer moved to the marshal's side and gripped his arm.

'Th-that's him, M-Marshal Fallen,' he stammered. 'That's the critter that tried to kill me and put a bullet in the judge.'

Fallen narrowed his eyes.

'Maybe,' he drawled.

'It's him, I tell you,' Elmer insisted angrily.

'Hold your horses. That's just a galoot wearing a black hat and coat, Elmer,' Fallen said. He was squinting in a vain attempt to see the concealed face of the man standing in the middle of the stage. 'We never saw the face of the shooter. That fella up there could be anyone.'

'Matt's right, Elmer,' Doc agreed. 'You gotta be certain before you go off half-cocked accusing folks.'

11

Just like everyone else inside the Tivoli, Matt Fallen and his two companions were bemused by the sight of the great illusionist as he came to a halt five feet from the footlights. But for the lawmen there was a different reason for their interest. They were wondering if their suspicions about the strange figure were correct or not.

You could have heard a pin drop in the auditorium as the entire audience held its breath and watched the black-clad man in front of them.

For a moment nothing happened.

The dimmed lamps cast a chilling, shadowy light upon the figure as, standing with his head bowed, he slowly raised his arm.

Suddenly a cloud of smoke engulfed him. The smoke startled the onlookers: open-mouthed, they watched as it rose to the Tivoli's vaulted ceiling.

As the dense cloud dispersed the hat and large black cape fell to the ground in a pile. The audience gasped. Men rose from their seats and stared at the empty clothing. A hundred voices could be heard asking one another what had happened. None of them was given a satisfactory answer.

Then the overhead lanterns suspended above the stage trained their illumination on something moving out of the depths of the shadows towards the front of the stage.

The small band began playing again.

The Tivoli was now filled with the rustling sound of unease.

The music grew louder. Excited anticipation had turned to fear of the unknown as the ghostly shapes slowly ventured towards the footlights. The five musicians in the orchestra pit gave a rousing drum roll to announce the final act on the Tivoli's first night.

The proud owner of the Tivoli, Willard Parker, stepped out from the side curtains, gestured to the centre of his stage and announced:

'Ladies and gentlemen, the Tivoli is proud to present all the way from the Eastern seaboard, the incredible and mesmerizing Mezmo the Great.'

Parker retreated behind the curtains as soon as his short speech was over. Fevered applause erupted as the musicians began to heighten the expectation.

From the depths of the shadows on the stage a seven-foot-high cabinet was slowly pushed forwards by two burly stagehands. The cabinet came to a stop just a few feet from the footlights.

The stagehands hastily exited stage left, leaving the cabinet bathed in the lights that surrounded it. The crowd stared at the large box, clapping and whistling.

It was like looking at an upright coffin to the eyes of those who until now had only read stories about the mysterious Mezmo. Every member of the audience had a different notion of what would happen next.

None of them was correct.

For Mezmo never simply gave his audience what they expected. That was too easy. Mezmo would delight, horrify and amaze those who watched him work. He would leave them forever mystified by what they had witnessed during his act. And, as with all of his profession, he would never divulge the secrets of his legendary illusions.

Legend had it that Mezmo was no simple magician but a psychic practitioner who could actually do the impossible. They believed all the dime novel stories which they had read before his arrival in War Smoke. Nearly the entire audience were convinced the great Mezmo was capable of doing real magic, for they were unable to imagine how, otherwise, complicated illusions were created and performed.

The music grew louder and more unsettling for a few moments. When the audience could barely take any more of the pulsating chords that filled the Tivoli they saw two shadowy figures walking towards the centre of the stage and the cabinet.

Both figures were clad in black.

'What in tarnation's going on, Marshal Fallen?' the confused Elmer whispered into the lawman's ear.

'Damned if I know, boy.' Fallen shook his head and his unblinking eyes continued to watch the two figures as they moved towards the tall cabinet.

Gasps spread around the auditorium as the audience caught sight of the two artistes. The beautiful female looked no more than twenty and was dressed in a long black gown which some said was actually greasepaint painted over her naked form. Her small left hand rested upon Mezmo's arm as they walked slowly towards the front of the stage.

The famed hypnotist was clad in a hand-tailored suit with a dark cape draped over his shoulders. Mezmo was just short of six foot in height with a well-groomed mane of silver hair and an impressive moustache.

It was impossible for any of those

who looked upon the famed showman to judge exactly how old he was or what he actually looked, like for Mezmo's features were hidden beneath thick layers of greasepaint.

The pair stopped in front of the cabinet and gave a gentle bow to those who had paid dearly to see them. Then, in a grand gesture, Mezmo pulled the cape from his shoulders and twirled it like a matador for a few moments.

For the very first time since the show had started Drew Clancy paused in his drinking and looked at the stage. His eyes focused on Mezmo as the famed mesmerist continued to spin his cape. The gambler rubbed his eyes, then returned his attention to his whiskey.

Athletically, Mezmo tossed the heavy cape upwards. To the astonishment of the entire audience it seemed to vanish into thin air. Again gasps sounded in the Tivoli as those in the crowded room tried to make sense of what they had just seen.

None of the audience had ever

witnessed anything like it before, but the show had only just started. The man who had become famous for his ability to make others fall helplessly under his hypnotic spells moved around the stage before returning to where his lovely assistant waited.

Mezmo pointed a finger at his assistant and then moved around her as she remained totally motionless. She stood like a statue bathed in the flattering light of one of the overhead lights.

Yet no sculptor had ever carved as beautiful a statue as Victoria Vale. She was breathtaking and had every single member of the audience staring at her in awe. Men of every class found themselves wanting to make love to her while the female members of the crowd simply wanted to be her.

Victoria remained perfectly still as Mezmo moved around her slim figure. The great mesmerist seemed to be spinning an invisible web around his assistant, though all those present in the Tivoli were convinced that its threads actually existed.

His fingers gently pulled at the air and she moved as though she were nothing more than a mere puppet. But the web was not just controlling Victoria, it was controlling the onlookers too.

Mezmo made several windmill gestures with his arms as his fingers moved like crawling spiders before her beautiful eyes.

Then he turned to face the crowd. Mezmo looked at them and raised both his hands into the air.

To the surprise of everyone in the Tivoli Victoria began to elevate off the boards. Only a few inches at first, then more than a yard up into the air. Mezmo continued to wave his arms around, as if she were a marionette and he the puppet master.

Victoria slowly moved above the audience like a ghost.

'This, my dear friends, is my protégée Victoria,' Mezmo announced. Then, with a flourish he added, 'She will transport us into the darkest recesses of our minds.

The fortunate will return but those who have black souls may disappear for ever and never return. Victoria has the power to mystify, for she is unlike ordinary females. Victoria has been blessed with gifts few others can even imagine. Only I, Mezmo the Great, have the power to control her many incredible gifts. Tonight we shall amaze you. Tonight we shall let you see things that no one has ever seen before.'

Mezmo looked at the audience. 'If you are brave enough, my friends, travel with us into the unknown.'

Matt Fallen lowered his beer glass, glanced at Doc and leaned down to his friend.

'It seems to me that I recognize that critter's voice, Doc,' he said. He stared through the cigar smoke at the stage. 'I'm sure that I've heard it before.'

'That ain't possible, Matt,' Doc told him. He took a sip of his beer. 'That Mezmo *hombre* only just arrived in War Smoke in the last couple of days. I'll bet you he ain't ever left New York before.'

The marshal scratched his jaw.

'I ain't so sure of that. He uses long fancy words but that ain't no Eastern accent, Doc,' the lawman commented. 'And I've got me a feeling I've heard it before.'

Doc looked curious. 'You have?'

Before Fallen could answer, Elmer pushed between his older companions in order to get an unobstructed view of the stage.

'Will you two galoots hush up?' he scolded. 'I wanna see this.'

Matt Fallen grinned and leaned on the bar counter. He lifted his beer glass to his mouth and was about to finish the last of his suds when he saw Drew Clancy move away from the counter, walk to the aisle and into the shadowy crowd. The marshal scratched his cheek with his thumbnail thoughtfully.

Doc looked at the tall lawman. 'What's the matter, Matt?'

Fallen looked troubled.

'I ain't sure, Doc,' he answered. He handed a half-dozen silver dollars to the medical man. 'You and Elmer enjoy the rest of the show on me.'

'Where you going?' Doc asked.

Fallen straightened his Stetson.

'I'm just heading over to my office for a little while to take a look at some of my old Wanted posters, Doc,' he replied. 'There's something I've gotta check out.'

Doc Weaver watched as the lawman strode unnoticed out of the Tivoli towards his office.

Elmer glanced at Doc and grinned excitedly.

'What do you figure that Mezmo's gonna do next, Doc?' he asked.

The seasoned medical man considered the question for a few seconds and then sighed wryly.

'He's gonna make an elephant appear out of that cabinet, Elmer,' Doc guessed, and grinned. 'What else?'

But it was no elephant that the mesmerist produced from his inside pocket. It was a .22 calibre gun. Mezmo held the small pistol in one hand while his other appeared to guide the floating female over the heads of the stunned crowd.

Then to the utter surprise and shock of everyone in the Tivoli Mezmo aimed and fired the small-calibre gun at the floating Victoria. The gunsmoke had barely left the barrel of his weapon when everyone realized that the attractive assistant had vanished.

'Do not concern yourselves, my friends,' Mezmo announced, standing in the centre of the stage. 'I have sent Victoria to the afterlife, but soon I shall bring her back. Then and only then shall you witness something few others have ever experienced. You shall encounter the impossible.'

12

The sky above War Smoke had grown darker as thunderous clouds drifted across the sprawling settlement and growled like ravenous cougars. Flashes of blinding venom splintered down from the brooding sky as the marshal moved quickly across the wide street. The lawman paused for a moment and stared up at the sky as a forked bolt of lightning briefly lit up the town. It was as though the legendary gods were warning him of even more danger.

The lawman removed his hat and mopped the beads of sweat off his brow with his sleeve. He wondered whether the killing had ended, or had the slaying of the four wealthy card players just been the beginning of something even more horrific.

Another flash of bright lightning streaked across the overhead darkness.

His eyes darted to where he had caught a glimpse of the white explosion and watched in awe as the further explosions raced across the heavens.

A chill traced his backbone.

The marshal exhaled and turned towards his office door. His large hand inserted the key into the lock and twisted it. He pushed the door inward and entered the dimly lit room.

Matt Fallen tossed his hat up on to the hat stand and pulled out his chair. He sat down at his desk and started going through the large pile of old posters once again. This time he was not distracted by his ever-talkative deputy.

Most of the images on the circulars were so crude that they could have been of anyone, but a few had photographic likenesses that Fallen recognized.

He thumbed through them and began to notice one similarity they all shared. Most of the wanted men he was looking at were already dead. Some had fallen foul of the posse's bullets while others had died of various causes in prison. Quite a lot had gone to meet their Maker as they plied their deadly trade.

A few, though, had somehow vanished.

That intrigued the lawman as he continued to study the pile of posters spread out before him on his desk. How, he wondered, could anyone with a price on his head simply disappear?

Fallen continued to wonder as he worked his way through the old posters.

After only five minutes Fallen found the poster his craw had been nagging him about ever since the killing had started in War Smoke.

Fallen sat back in his chair with the circular in his hands and silently read the words printed upon its browning surface.

'This has to be it,' he mumbled to himself. He rose to his feet, carefully folded the poster and slid it into his shirt. 'If I'm right the killing is about to stop.'

Fallen walked around his desk, plucked his Stetson off the hat stand and placed it over his dark hair. He locked the office up and stepped out into the street.

As the lawman turned his broad shoulders his gaze darted up and down the familiar street. There were far fewer folks out than normal, he thought.

He patted his flat belly. He could feel the poster against his skin as he stepped down on to the sand and began crossing Front Street. With each stride of his long legs the lawman considered his options. There were many ways he could go about getting his hands on the deadly killer who had terrorized War Smoke since sundown.

As he eased his wide frame between the scores of abandoned buggies left filling the street his hands carefully made sure that his .45 was fully loaded. He plucked spent casings from his weapon's chambers and replaced them with fresh bullets from his gunbelt.

By the time the marshal had reached the opposite side of Front Street the seven-inch-barrelled Peacemaker was fully loaded. Fallen dropped the gun back into its holster and stepped up on to the boardwalk.

He paused between a pair of flaming torches.

Fallen knew that the only way the killer could be stopped was for him to put lead into the man before he somehow got the drop on anyone else.

Fallen sighed deeply and marched back into the Tivoli. No one attempted to stop Matt Fallen when he had a full head of steam up and blowing.

Fallen made his way back into the saloon and walked to where he had left his two friends. He rested a boot on the brass floor rail and leaned his hip against the counter.

Doc pushed a full beer glass towards him.

'Thanks, Doc.' He nodded. His eyes stared at the solitary Mezmo up on the stage. Fallen raised an eyebrow and took a mouthful of beer.

'You weren't long, Matt,' Doc remarked.

'Nope, I found what I was looking for real quick, Doc,' the marshal told him. He lowered the beer glass from his mouth.

Doc glanced keenly up at the lawman. 'What was you looking for in a pile of old circulars, Matt boy?'

'The name of the killer,' Fallen drawled.

'You know who the killer is, boy?' Doc gasped.

'I think so.' Fallen took another swallow of the cool amber beer. 'I'll wait for the show to end and then go and find out.'

'How in tarnation do you reckon on finding out, Matt?' Doc asked. 'You can't just walk up to a critter and say 'excuse me, are you the fella that's bin killing folks?' Can you?'

Fallen cast his eyes down to the elderly doctor.

'Why not, Doc?' he asked.

Doc Weaver shrugged. 'Damned if I know.'

★   ★   ★

With the audience in the palm of his hand, Mezmo the Great continued to whet their appetite as he used every inch of the stage to his advantage. He had performed five startling illusions since he had made the beautiful Victoria vanish in a cloud of gunsmoke, but now he knew that it was time to bring her back from the afterlife.

With every eye in the Tivoli glued to his expert hands the famed Mezmo raised his arms and slowly lowered his head as though he were falling under one of his own spells.

'Now it is time, Victoria,' he called out. 'Time for your return to the land of the living.'

Once again the crowd gasped in awe and disbelief as Mezmo pointed down at two members of the front row and gestured for them to come up on stage.

'If you two gentlemen will come up here for a moment,' Mezmo said as the men mounted the wooden steps to the stage. 'Please check the cabinet closely. Inspect it to ensure that it's empty.'

The two men did as they were commanded and thoroughly checked the large wooden box. One of the pair stepped up to the famed Mezmo and grinned bashfully.

'There ain't nobody or nothing in that there box, mister,' he said. Mezmo bowed to the two of them.

'I thank you, gentlemen,' he said and pointed for them to return to their seats. Then, with a flourish, Mezmo swung around and pointed at the cabinet. A large puff of smoke rose up in front of the tall box. As the smoke cleared the beautiful Victoria could be seen, seated inside it.

'Behold, Victoria has returned.' Mezmo held out a hand and led Victoria out of the cabinet. She gave a gentle bow as the box was pushed off the stage, leaving only Mezmo and herself on the boards.

None of the crowd had ever seen anything like this before and they liked what they were witnessing. The mesmerist took out the small gun again and handed it to his assistant.

'Now, my friends,' he said. 'Now you will see my lovely Victoria show what an expert she is with a gun.'

Mezmo pointed to a place on the far side of the stage. Victoria walked to the spot, then turned to face him. He took a deck of playing cards out of his vest pocket. He shuffled the cards, then looked at Victoria.

'Are you ready, my dear?' he called across to her. 'Are you ready to do the impossible?'

'I'm ready, Mezmo,' she replied. She held the gun at arm's length.

He made a flamboyant gesture to the watching crowd.

'Victoria is nearly ready, my friends,' Mezmo announced. 'She will shoot cards out of the air while in a mesmerized trance. Her eyes will be closed tightly but she will still see them and, with uncanny accuracy, Victoria will shoot them down.'

The crowd all gasped as one as, taking in his words, they began to fret about his safety. Their troubled eyes glanced from one side of the stage to the other as they observed the two totally different figures.

Mezmo stared straight at Victoria and waved his hand in rhythmic motion. The young blonde's head began to sway and her eyes closed. Once again the ultimate illusionist was controlling her with the aid of invisible strings. Although they stood at opposite sides of the stage it was as if they were joined together. Mezmo glanced at the audience.

'Do not fret about what you are about to witness, my friends,' he told them as he stood squarely opposite his young assistant. 'Victoria is an expert shot when mesmerized. Note that her eyes are closed tightly. The spirits will guide her bullets.'

Mezmo was defying all known laws of physics and none of the crowd had any inkling as to how he was achieving the miraculous feat.

Faster than the finest card-sharp could ever hope to deal a deck, Mezmo began spinning cards up into the air. As the cards span into the illumination of the lights, Victoria began firing the gun.

Each shot was as accurate as the last. The first five cards were indeed plucked from the air just as Mezmo had predicted. Then Victoria paused while Mezmo took a bow.

As Mezmo straightened up and glanced at the smoking six-shooter in her hand a wicked grin appeared on his heavily made-up face.

He held a playing card against his shirt front and then turned to face Victoria.

'You have a bullet remaining, my dear,' he said loudly. 'Use it.'

The entranced beauty did exactly as her master instructed her and squeezed the trigger one last time.

The great Mezmo was the target.

Once again Victoria did not miss her target. The stunned audience watched the unmistakable flash of the bullet leaving the gun barrel. It tapered across the stage faster than a sidewinder's strike.

A cloud of choking smoke enveloped the mesmerist.

When it dispersed the famed Mezmo was nowhere to be seen. The bewildered crowd stood stunned in disbelief as they tried to work out where the mesmerist had gone.

Victoria remained on the side of the stage, motionless, holding the smoking .22 in her small hand.

Then, to the utter surprise of the onlookers, the crumpled black hat and cape started to rise slowly from the floor. With every heartbeat the hat and cape rose higher and higher before their very eyes.

Then it stopped.

Mezmo removed the floppy-brimmed hat, bowed and snapped his fingers in the direction of his assistant. The cheering was deafening as the audience expressed their relief. Victoria appeared to reawaken at the sound. She ran to his side and joined hands with him.

They bowed and stepped backwards.

The heavy satin curtains fell from either side of the stage and the two performers disappeared from sight. The music continued as one by one the crowd gathered their belongings and started to leave the Tivoli.

Matt Fallen looked at his deputy and then to Doc. He thumbed his jawline and lifted his beer to his mouth.

'You'd best hang around in here, Doc,' Fallen said, wiping the suds from his lips. 'Your services might be needed.' He placed the glass down on the counter and looked at his deputy.

'C'mon, Elmer,' he drawled. 'We're going backstage.'

'What for, Marshal Fallen?' Elmer asked. He picked up his shotgun and tucked it under his arm.

Matt Fallen gritted his teeth and narrowed his eyes as he led his deputy down one of the aisles.

'You wanna get that varmint that put a hole in your best vest, don't you?' the tall marshal drawled as he negotiated a route towards the stage.

Elmer's eyes darted nervously about him and he gripped his shotgun even more tightly in his hands.

'I reckon so.' He gulped. 'I might not be so lucky the next time he shoots at me, though.'

Fallen paused and looked down into Elmer's trusting face. He understood the deputy's anxiety.

'I want you to remain out here with your shotgun, Elmer,' the marshal said. He patted the youngster's shoulder. 'If you hear shooting coming from backstage I want you to stay here in case the varmint tries to escape this way. Savvy?'

Elmer gulped again, harder this time. 'How will I know the killer? I surely don't wanna shoot an innocent critter, Marshal.'

'Shoot anyone that comes out running with a smoking gun in his hand, Elmer,' Fallen instructed him. 'You might be the last chance War Smoke's got against this crazy galoot. You might be all that stands between it and a bloodbath, boy.'

Before the shaking deputy could open his mouth again, the broad-shouldered marshal had made his way backstage to find the man he suspected of being the ruthless killer.

Twitching, Elmer slowly rested his bony shoulder against the wall and held the doubled-barrelled shotgun in his shaking hands.

'I'm the town's last chance.' He repeated the marshal's words and nodded at Doc, who was standing beside the bar counter. Elmer wiped the sweat off his face and forced a smile for his wrinkled friend. 'War Smoke might be in a whole heap of trouble by my reckoning.'

Finale

Behind the heavy stage curtains the backstage area was virtually empty. The stagehands had left to find beer and whiskey that now they could actually afford, while most of the show's entertainers had departed from the Tivoli, going for the numerous saloons and eateries dotted around town. They had not waited for the great Mezmo to finish his act.

The backstage area was in shadow as Matt Fallen cautiously made his way through the clutter of props and scenery to where he knew he would find the man he sought.

With every step Fallen recalled bit by bit the last part of the act, which he had watched after returning to the Tivoli. Although he was convinced that Mezmo had to be the ruthless killer who had plagued War Smoke since sundown, the sight of Victoria Vale using the .22 calibre handgun kept gnawing at his craw.

He had seldom seen anyone capable of hitting spinning playing cards before, but the young blonde had done so with ease. For someone to achieve this feat with their eyes closed seemed impossible, but he had watched the attractive Victoria, who had somehow managed to do it.

Not once but five times in breathtaking succession.

Fallen began to wonder if she was the killer.

Victoria had done what the deadly killer had achieved: she had hit her targets with unerring accuracy. But the figure he and Elmer had exchanged bullets with in the dark lane earlier had appeared to be of far bigger build than the delicate female, he thought.

Or was even that just another illusion created by the wizardly mesmerist? Had they only seen what Mezmo wanted them to see?

Maybe the black cape and large hat

had simply played tricks with their eyes and their minds. Was that it? Fallen wondered if he could trust anything he saw in this strange world he was heading more deeply into.

The tall lawman carefully made his way between stacked wooden boards to where he could see a pool of dim lamplight.

Fallen began to doubt his own theory about whom he was actually hunting. The lawman ducked beneath a series of dangling ropes and continued on towards the amber light. He was being drawn towards it like a moth, but he knew that somewhere ahead he would find the answers he sought. What had seemed like a watertight theory in his office when he had found the Wanted poster now appeared to be filled with holes.

The marshal carefully moved around some scenery and then stopped. This backstage foray had taken him far longer than he had planned because of the near-darkness, but now he was looking straight at the line of dressing-rooms.

They were all abandoned apart from the one used by Mezmo and his assistant. Fallen stared at its closed door. He could hear muffled voices behind it.

He rested the palm of his hand on the grip of his holstered gun. The last thing he wanted to do was draw his seven-inch-barrelled Colt on an innocent party, but he knew that the person he hunted was a deadly shot. The killer could expertly put a bullet into a man's heart even in the gloom of a shadowy lane. The marshal cautiously strode through the half-light towards the dressing-room and rapped his knuckles across its fresh paintwork.

'I know you're in there, Mezmo,' he shouted. 'Open up.'

To his surprise the door opened and he was faced with the beautiful young female. She looked up into his eyes and smiled gently. Without uttering a single word Victoria turned to where Mezmo was seated in front of a mirror. Fallen eased her aside and stared at the reflection in the mirror. It was a very different face from the one he had seen on stage. The moustache was gone and so were most of the wrinkles. The white hair was now dark.

Matt Fallen frowned in confusion.

'You've discovered my secret, Marshal Fallen.' Mezmo turned and wiped the remains of the greasepaint from his features. Then his burning eyes stared up at the looming lawman. 'I look slightly different without my stage make-up.'

Fallen tilted his head. 'But you're still the critter I'm looking for.'

Mezmo smiled. 'Of course. I am Mezmo the Great.'

The marshal shook his head gently. His eyes glanced across the hands of both Mezmo and Victoria in case either of them should suddenly produce a deadly .22 and start shooting.

'No you ain't. You're Frank Warner,' Fallen contradicted. 'You were convicted and sentenced to death for the killing of your wife five years back. I heard tell of you escaping, but why

179

would you come back here?'

The sound of a violent storm rumbled over the roof of the Tivoli. Mezmo stared hard into the marshal's eyes.

'You are wrong, Marshal,' he said.

Fallen swiftly drew his gun and cocked its hammer. He kept it trained on the seated performer.

'There are two reasons why I know that you are really Frank Warner, Mezmo,' he drawled. 'One is that I recognize your voice and the other is that you made the mistake of calling me by my name. I haven't said who I am but you called me Marshal Fallen anyway.'

Mezmo stood up and gave a bow. 'You were a fine jailer, Fallen. The finest and most honourable man that I've ever met but you allowed me to be rail-roaded.'

Fallen raised an eyebrow. 'What d'you mean?'

'I never killed my wife.' Mezmo sighed. 'But someone in this fair town did. There was money involved in her murder and the same money bought me a one-way ticket to the gallows. Had I not escaped I would now be six feet underground.'

'You claiming you were innocent?' Fallen asked.

'Yes. I'm innocent.' Mezmo lifted his coat off a chair and draped it around his shoulders. 'The true killer has paid for his crimes, though. He and his friends have paid with their lives for what they did.'

Matt Fallen stared at Mezmo. 'So you admit you killed Holt Berkley, Lou Franklin, Seth Gordon and Jed Silver?'

'Not I, Marshal.' Mezmo patted Victoria on her slender shoulders. 'Someone else killed them for me. A willing and able person.'

Matt Fallen aimed his gun nervously at Victoria Vale.

'So you killed them for Mezmo,' he stated. 'Reckon you'd best put a coat over them shoulders, ma'am. I'm taking you both to jail.'

Mezmo shook his head. 'Victoria did not kill those four bastards, Marshal. She is simply my assistant. The person you want is someone else. Someone who is very close at this precise moment, in fact.'

'What?' Fallen backed away from the dressing-room door and glanced around the shadows. 'Are you telling me that you've got some critter spellbound? Where is he?'

'He's closer than you think, Marshal.'

Fallen was uneasy. 'Keep talking, Mezmo.'

'You see, I am indeed one of the best mesmerists in the country but even I cannot put someone in a trance if they are strong-willed like yourself.' Mezmo shrugged. 'Victoria is a simple subject. I can control her quite easily. You on the other hand are impossible to hypnotize.'

'I ain't flattered.' Matt Fallen kept looking around the backstage area of the Tivoli nervously. 'Are you telling me that you put someone in town under your spell and got him to do your killing for you? Is that even possible?'

'It is given the right subject.' Mezmo smiled. 'I found someone in town only two hours after we arrived, Marshal. He was pliable to my will and of a murderous nature. It was simple.'

Suddenly, out in the depths of the shadowy scenery a sound caught the lawman's keen hearing. Fallen swung around with his six-shooter gripped firmly in his hand.

'Show yourself,' Fallen shouted.

The tall lawman stared in disbelief as he watched Drew Clancy move out of the gloom towards him. He was about to ask Mezmo if the infamous gambler was the killer when the great illusionist smashed two glass balls on the ground. They exploded and filled the backstage area with a dense fog. Smoke continued to billow up from the shattered glass. It filled the air as a bullet came tapering through the choking mist from Clancy's gun. The bullet ripped the hat from the lawman's head.

Fallen hastily crouched, pulled on his trigger and returned fire.

Two more shots whistled through the smoke and narrowly missed the lawman as he took cover behind the wall of the dressing-room and fired again. Red flashes of lethal fury hit the wooden wall. A thousand splinters rained over the lawman.

After the exchange lead through the haze and shadows the smoke cleared enough for both men to be able to see one another. Clancy had no expression on his face as he fired again. A chunk of wood was ripped from the doorframe two inches above the lawman's head.

This was no time for finesse. Fallen fanned his gunhammer and sent his remaining bullets in the direction of the approaching gambler.

The marshal watched as Drew Clancy was knocked off his feet and fell in a heap on to his back. Blood poured from the holes in the now lifeless gambler's fancy shirt front. Fallen quickly reloaded and looked around the dressing-room for the two performers.

To his utter surprise both Mezmo and Victoria had vanished. Fallen spun on his boot heel in a vain attempt to catch a glimpse of the couple. Then he spotted that the stagedoor was ajar.

The lawman dashed to the stage door and pushed it open. He stumbled outside into the alley and looked along its dark length for any sign of either Mezmo or the beautiful Victoria.

There was still no sign of them.

Fallen raced along the side of the Tivoli to Front Street and skidded to a halt. Scores of buggies were making their way slowly out of the heart of town. Frustrated, the lawman rubbed his lips with the back of his hand. He narrowed his eyes and made his way to the front of the saloon. He had only just reached the entrance of the Tivoli when a thunderclap erupted in the heavens above him. He instinctively ducked as Doc meandered out of the Tivoli with his thumbs in his vest pockets.

'What's wrong, Matt?' he asked wryly.

A lonesome train whistle then sounded on the air. Matt Fallen stretched up to his full height and caught a glimpse of the night train leaving the rail depot fifty yards away down the main thorough-fare. Smoke trailed up into the brooding sky as flashes of lightning splintered across the heavens.

'Damn it all!' Fallen cursed and rested his rump on the saloon's hitching rail. He shook his head in defeat and holstered his gun.

'What's eating you, Matt?' Doc asked.

The weary marshal looked into the wrinkled face of his oldest friend and shrugged.

'I got me a gut feeling that the *hombre* behind all the killings has just left War Smoke, Doc,' he said, and sighed.

'So the killer has got away, huh?' Doc raised his bushy eyebrows. 'Don't fret, Matt boy. You did your best.'

Fallen scratched his head.

'No, Doc. You don't understand. I shot the killer,' he said enigmatically.

'Then who got away?'

'Mezmo and that pretty gal of his,' Fallen replied wearily. 'Mezmo put Drew Clancy under his spell and got that gambler to kill Holt and his buddies. Mezmo's real name's Frank Warner. He reckoned Holt and the others killed his wife and got him sentenced to hang.'

Doc looked confused but he patted his tall pal on the back sympathetically. 'I reckon you surely need some shuteye, son. You're starting to talk gibberish.'

Fallen exhaled. 'Maybe you're right, Doc. I am kinda tired now you mention it. Reckon I'll go and take me a long sleep in the jail and when I wake up I'll explain the whole story to you.'

Doc was about to amble away when the lawman looked over his shoulder at the medical man.

'That reminds me, Doc. There's another dead 'un out back of this damn place. Go take a look at his carcass and then we'll tally up on how much money you're owed.'

Doc lifted his hat. 'Much obliged, Matthew. This has bin the most profitable night I've had in years.'

'Think nothing of it, old friend.' Matt Fallen yawned as he steered his boots towards his office. 'Happy to oblige.'

'Should I tell Elmer he can relax now, Matt?' Doc asked.

Matt Fallen turned his head and smiled wickedly. 'Not until sunup, Doc. Not until sunup.'

We do hope that you have enjoyed reading this large print book.

Did you know that all of our titles are available for purchase?

We publish a wide range of high quality large print books including:
Romances, Mysteries, Classics
General Fiction
Non Fiction and Westerns

Special interest titles available in large print are:
The Little Oxford Dictionary
Music Book, Song Book
Hymn Book, Service Book

Also available from us courtesy of Oxford University Press:
Young Readers' Dictionary
(large print edition)
Young Readers' Thesaurus
(large print edition)

For further information or a free brochure, please contact us at:
Ulverscroft Large Print Books Ltd.,
The Green, Bradgate Road, Anstey,
Leicester, LE7 7FU, England.
Tel: (00 44) **0116 236 4325**
Fax: (00 44) **0116 234 0205**

A RETURN TO THE ALAMO

Paul Bedford

British Army deserter Thomas Collins is working with the Texas Rangers to bring supplies of gunpowder back to San Antonio for the continuing struggle against the fearsome Comanche Nation. As they slowly drive their heavy-laden wagons back, Thomas's past catches up with him in the form of a ruthless British officer, Captain Speirs, who has crossed the Atlantic to apprehend him. Thomas must take control of the Rangers if they are to reach San Antonio safely, but he faces some tough decisions when his lover Sarah is kidnapped by Speirs . . .

GUNFIGHT AT HILTON'S CROSSING

Bill Cartwright

Drifter Chuck Mellors is wondering where his next dollar will come from when he receives an enticing proposition from an unpleasant man. Inveigled into assisting in a robbery which goes terribly wrong, he soon becomes a fugitive from the law. Seeking justice not only for himself, but also for the widow and child who are suffering as a consequence of the crime, Chuck Mellors embarks upon a long journey through the Indian Territories to Texas. Here, in the little town of Hilton's Crossing, matters reach a shocking and deadly resolution.

BLACKWATER

Abe Dancer

When Jack Rogan decides to return home from years of gambling on the Mississippi riverboats, he makes a mistake by taking what he thinks is a shorter, faster route back to Texas. The Louisiana swamplands are teeming with danger, not least Gaston Savoy, Homer Lamb and their kin from the secluded waterside community of Whistler. Captured and stripped of money, guns and his mare, Jack is compromised into making a deal with his captors. Soon, he discovers the real reason for his internment — and just what is expected of him.